A Jury of Peers

All characters appearing in this work are fictitious. Any resemblance to real persons, living or dead, is purely coincidental.

Publisher: White Schoolhouse Publishing LLC

ISBN: 0984699708
ISBN-13: 9780984699704

Cover Photography: Stephen Taylor

"No freeman shall be seized, or imprisoned, or dispossessed, or outlawed, or in any way destroyed; nor will we condemn him, nor will we commit him to prison, excepting by the legal judgement of his peers, or by the laws of the land."

Magna Carta, or the Great Charter of King John granted June 15, 1215.

CHAPTER ONE

She eyed the palisades across the river, fading in the failing sunlight. Old Judge, a craggy face worn into the limestone bluffs, peered back at her through the kitchen window. With the lengthening shadows Rebecca Millington's thoughts were passing from the cares of the day to night's promise of peace and quiet.

Another day gone by and not much to show for it. Momma's asleep. Better get Junie ready for bed...

As she turned to call her little boy's name a rush of alarm surged through the weary mother.

Junie's not home!

Four-year-old James Millington, Junior, was her only child and the namesake of his daddy, dead in a car wreck more than a year ago.

Rebecca scurried toward the ramshackle house trailer squatting like a speckled toad behind her neat white cottage. Cora Lee Patton, called Corly, her brother Matthew's wife, hunkered on the trailer's cinder block stoop, her bowed head framed by a flicker from inside.

"I've come to fetch my Junie. I was tending to Momma and sent him down after supper to play with your Billy Joe."

Corly choked a response behind a clenched jaw and did not raise her eyes. Eight-year-old Billy Joe was the eldest of her and Matthew's three children and their only son. She was used to his being gone past dark and complained little – that was between the boy and his father – but the set of her body betrayed her anxiety. He had gone off down the river with his little cousin and they had not yet come home.

The screen door burst open and Matthew, naked to the waist, pushed past his wife into the yard. His red-webbed eyes bulged from deep-set sockets. One hand clutched a sweating beer can; the other cupped an ash-tipped cigarette. Lean and edgy as a banty rooster, he was the physical and emotional opposite of his plump and placid sister. Their father's dark, sharp-boned features seemed their sole common trait. But for self-neglect, he might be considered handsome, she fetching, in a common sort of way.

Matthew shuffled a jittery sidestep, alternating swigs of beer with quick puffs on the cigarette, then spewed a raspy tirade. "You got to look after them kids all the goddam time! I told that little fart he better get home before dark, him havin' Junie with him and all. That boy's been nothin' but aggravation since school let out. He won't mind no matter how hard I switch him. He just gives me the meanest damn look, just like our daddy did when he got mad. Like he wants to whip me. You know what I mean, Rebecca? Only time he's happy's when he goes down by the river or just doin' what he wants."

He sucked in a lungful of smoke, held it for a long moment then blew a stale cloud upon which rode the rest of his plaint. "Lord knows I try to be a good daddy what with the hard times and no work and all. You know what I mean, Rebecca, you know what I mean? Just like our daddy liked it best when he was doin' what he wanted and didn't want to be around Momma or us kids."

Matthew Patton loved to pour out his woes. His wife and sister had heard it all before and were unmoved. They knew whatever he said would be a version of reality in which he was free of blame.

2

The man glanced toward the river disappearing into the gloom. The sun's last glow hung before his face, wrapping him in a russet haze, then crashed into pitch-blackness behind the palisades. The rant ended as abruptly as spill from a dam when the sluice gate shuts.

Matthew turned to face the women. Soothed by the darkness, he took up again in less strident tones. "Well, they's likely left the river this late. Probably chasin' lightnin' bugs over at Bobby Ray Caslow's or maybe by his daddy's shed. Otis's bitch got some puppies they's fixin' to drown if nobody takes 'em. I told Billy Joe we don't need no more mouths to feed, 'specially no mongrel dog. You know what I mean, don't you? They's too many of 'em runnin' around loose already. You know what I mean?"

"No matter where they are, it isn't where they ought to be," Rebecca said. The more Matthew talked the more he fed her growing apprehension. "Hadn't we better go look for them?"

Her question hung in the cloying air.

"Corly, you and Rebecca call down to Caslow's, see if you can find them boys! I'll drive up to Raymond's store, fetch'em if they's there. Prob'ly run into 'em on the way. I need some more Bud and Marlboros, anyhow. You know what I mean? Save me a trip tomorrow."

In motion before the words were out, Matthew drained the beer can, crushed it in his bony hand and tossed it onto a pile among its battered brothers. He took a long drag and flipped the butt, its tip blazing a neon arc into the void. He ducked into the trailer and came out seconds later, wearing an unbuttoned short-sleeve shirt. Jangling keys had replaced the cigarette in his right hand and a fresh can of brew filled the left.

Matthew headed toward a piebald blue pickup truck parked in the dirt behind the trailer, tried to start it and drew a grinding rumble. "The sonofabitch still won't turn over." He had been tinkering with the truck when he sent the boys off on their own.

3

"Rebecca, gimme your keys. I gotta take your Sentra."

Moments later, his sister's car gunned to a hard start, flung grit beneath its wheels like an angry bull, and roared away.

Through blurry eyes Rebecca stared the taillights into the distance.

She usually deferred to her brother, who at thirty-two was eight years older and head of the family by default. Matthew was the only surviving son and Rebecca the lone daughter of four live births and uncounted miscarriages. She had finished high school and a year of community college; he had reached the seventh grade when he quit school at sixteen.

Another time she might have cringed at her brother's abusing her car and her good nature. Tonight, she feared he might have put her only child in harm's way. Feelings of complicity overwhelmed her. She had sent Junie down by the river in her brother's care, knowing how irresponsible he could be. But she could not count on him to set it right. She would have to take matters into her hands.

Rebecca gathered her wits and raced to the riverbank, not sure which direction to take. *Where would Billy Joe take my Junie?* She started upriver where the channel narrowed coming out of a bend. *No! Current runs too fast up there! That's not where they'd play.* She turned around and picked her way through the clutter in the direction of The Point, a salient of land off which the river ran deepest, the most likely destination of little boys gone fishing.

"Junie! Billy Joe!"

"Billy Joe! Junie!"

Over and over she called out their names, her cries shattering on the dense night air like so many spun-glass beads. Minutes into her frenzied search the adrenaline rush began to ebb. She drew up, drenched in perspiration. Her sandal clad feet oozed blood from a dozen nicks. Insect bites pocked her bare skin. Tears poured from swollen eyes, sore from mining the gloom for traces of the little boys. She spun round and round in place, futile as a dog chasing its tail, and listened through labored breath for her baby's answering call.

I won't ever find my Junie this way! Maybe Matthew was right — even my worthless brother is right sometimes — they've left the river and gone down to Caslow's or up to Raymond's store.

The frantic mother stumbled with fresh resolve across a yard barely lit by the naked bulb above the back door, and into her kitchen. She punched familiar numbers into the phone and reached only a busy signal. She tried again, with the same distressing result. She started to have the operator cut in on the call, but a burst of optimism brought her down on the side of action. She would head to Caslow's on foot and, with luck, maybe run into the boys along the way. Rebecca toweled herself off and cleaned the cuts on her feet with alcohol, then exchanged the sandals for walking shoes.

Pearl Patton lay asleep on her back, a snore droning from her toothless mouth. She was just fifty-four, but worn out in mind and body, suffering from dementia, looking twenty years beyond her age. Like her daughter, she was a widow. Dander Patton had been stabbed to death a few years back. The police said he had been fighting over a floozy in a Lexington honky tonk. It was a comeuppance not unexpected for a man who took his pleasures wherever and whenever they could be found, fortified by bourbon whiskey, and who had treated his woes, both real and imagined, from the same bottle.

Corly was waiting when Rebecca came outside.

"I'm going down the road towards Missy's place to find those boys. You coming?" Rebecca said. Her tone carried more challenge than invitation.

"You know I can't leave those two little ones in there by themselves," Corly said, and nodded in the direction of the trailer where her daughters slept. She twisted strands of the bleached hair that hung limply across her bare, stooping shoulders. "Anyways, I don't see there's all that much to be bothered about. Billy Joe's just having a hard time right now, but he's a good boy and he loves your baby. Wouldn't let nothing happen to him."

Corly's forced optimism comforted neither woman.

"I'll call when I find them. You listen for my phone!" The words poured bitter as burnt coffee off Rebecca's tongue. Her baby should be asleep in his bed, not lost out in the dark.

As Rebecca walked away Corly said, "Matthew never told me Junie was with Billy Joe or I'd of been more worried. I went out with the girls right after supper. Sister Cadwell from the church come to take us to get some school clothes. I come home and he was lookin' at the TV, drinkin' beer. Didn't hardly say nothing and I know'd better than ask." If she were seeking sympathy or absolution, neither was to be found in her sister-in-law's heart.

Otis, pronounced with a short "O" in the manner of those parts, and Missy Caslow's doublewide trailer, palatial in contrast to Matthew Patton's sorry relic, perched on a swell more than a mile to the south, past The Point, away from the town. The two-lane roadbed ran roughly parallel to the course of the river and, having hardly any shoulder, forced a walker to keep to the scraggly grass and litter that bordered it.

It was now past nine on a Monday evening and little traffic passed along the road. The town and its outlying establishments were shut except for the taverns and convenience stores, and the gas station and fast food joints by the off-ramp. Rebecca kept a quick, steady pace despite the growing fatigue in her legs. An old farm truck passed her in the first ten minutes, heading south in the opposite lane, and sped up as it went by. She saw only the back of the driver's ball cap-covered head and couldn't tell if he was alone.

Is he trying to get away? Is he running off with my Junie?

She imagined the worst for her child then instantly recanted. New visions came in bright bursts: *He fell down! They drowned! No, not both of them.*

The boys got lost! No, Billy Joe knows the river good as anybody. Carried off by Gypsies! Yes, Gypsies. Everybody knows they take children to sell or raise for their own. No, no, they'll be inside Caslow's eating Missy's rhubarb pie and having a glass of Kool-Aid! Otis is getting ready to bring them home. They'll pass by here any minute now. Junie'll be asleep in the car. Matthew will find them at Raymond's store and whip Billy Joe for giving such a fright. But he'll bring my baby home!

The quarreling of dogs foraging along the riverbank sounded off to her right. She shuddered and conjured up yet another fearsome image.

Rebecca bypassed dwellings set close by the road or buried deeper in The Bottoms and barely visible. No comfort would be found there. For all they seemed outwardly to have in common, Tackers begrudged one another; their individual meanness grew in proportion to their collective decline. It was as bad on the east side of the road, a cultural divide of Mississippian proportions. The scanty farms and poor frame bungalows housed folk at best apathetic and more likely hostile to their river dwelling neighbors, alike in material want, but in little else.

Melissa and Otis Caslow were different. Missy grew up in Tackbottom, part of the prolific Taggert clan. The head of each generation had served as the unofficial ruler of the community, controlling the dole and bartering political clout. The wily Taggerts split their allegiance between the Blue and the Gray during the War Between the States, more by design than chance — their sympathies clearly were with the South. Opportunism was an abiding part of their nature. Afterwards, the division was quickly and quietly healed and the Union Taggerts reassimilated their Rebel kin.

Local lore had it that an early Taggert — his name lost in time — in his cups one afternoon shortly after the "reunion," imagined in the shadows of the bluffs across the river the face of a stern old man he was convinced was about to damn him for his evil ways. His taunting kin, no less under the influence of the corn than he, promptly dubbed the ominous wall the "Old

Judge." So far as anyone knew, the Taggert tippler awoke the next morning unpunished except for a ripping hangover, and took up again his ornery ways. The name, however, stuck and came over the years, almost to the point of reverence, to personify the palisades' dominance over the watershed.

Sim Taggert, the last patriarch and Missy Caslow's great uncle, had been fated to oversee the decline of influence in the years following World War II. Taggerts had lent their name to the community in successive corruptions from Taggert's Bottoms through Tag's Bottoms to simply Tackbottom or The Bottoms, but fewer of each succeeding generation stayed. As Taggert descendants left, an equally desperate lot took their places.

Otis Caslow was the son and grandson of coal miners who had come from Pike County to take a job in one of the small auto parts factories that sprang up on the fringes of the Bluegrass after Toyota built an assembly plant in Georgetown. His ancestral name had contained an additional syllable or two, but East European heritage had long since merged into Eastern Kentucky culture. He met Missy in the cafe where she waited table and moved with her to be among the vestiges of her family. The couple was hospitable and accepting. It was they and no blood relative of Rebecca Millington or her late husband who had looked after her, her feeble mother and her little boy in their difficult times of the past seventeen months.

Locked in the chaotic landscape of her mind, Rebecca failed to see an empty Coke bottle in her path. It rolled beneath her foot and tipped her sprawling forward. She braked with the heels of her hands and skidded in gravel and bits of broken glass. Off balance, she rolled, arms and legs flailing: a giant pale beetle flipped on its back.

Rebecca righted herself and lifted her bulk, intent on resuming her trek. She rubbed painful, gory palms across her flanks, all the while aiming an uncharacteristic stream of obscenities at no one and nothing in particular. It was, if unpleasant, at least a temporary distraction.

Not many more yards farther along she made out ahead the mercury vapor lamp glowing atop a pole at the front of Caslow's lot. Ordinarily, she would welcome that sight. Tonight she shivered despite the stifling heat as she prepared to cross the road.

Missy Caslow and six year old Bobby Ray sprawled on a brown tweed sofa, munching popcorn and watching television. A large window air conditioner poured cool air across their bodies. Otis sat at a Formica topped table in the tiny kitchen, papers spread in front of him, holding a telephone handset to one ear. Rebecca flinched as her tattered hand closed around the aluminum doorknob. She had put the fall out of her mind, but the effects persisted. She pushed the door open.

"Missy, it's me, Rebecca."

"Come in, woman, don't let the cool air out!" Missy said. None of the Caslows got up.

"I tried to call but your line was busy." Rebecca strained to be polite, then lost control. "Missy, Junie went out with Billy Joe after supper and they're still gone! Please say they've been here!"

"Why, no, Honey, they ain't here. I haven't seen them all day. Bobby Ray, you been playing with those boys?"

Her son nodded and looked up, sensing his answer would not please anyone. "Unh, Unh, Momma. Not since yesterday."

Rebecca collapsed onto the floor as despair crushed the last grain of hope.

The Pattons were waiting in the yard beside Rebecca's Nissan. Corly raised an arm to shield the glare of Otis's headlamps; tears glistened on her cheeks. Matthew leaned against the hood in his wife's shadow, wrapped in a private misery. He had not come upon the boys dawdling along the road or drinking soda pop or trading fish for candy at Raymond's store.

A burst of heat lightning laid bare the wretchedness of the creatures huddled below. The trailing crack of thunder drowned out for an instant the snarling of dogs along the riverbank.

CHAPTER TWO

Dale "Stubby" Carnahan was asleep when Sheriff Paul Tellis called to ask his help finding two lost Tacker kids. Stubby was Tellis's go-to deputy in the tiny department and on call for special cases.

"Okay, Sheriff. Yeah. I know it could be a waste of time. Who else will be there? The parents? Yeah, I understand. Yeah, I know. They vote, too. At Ott Caslow's? Yeah, I know where that is. An eight and a four year old? Damn! No, I'll be right out."

It was not a call he took gladly. The Bottoms was no place he wanted to be in the middle of the night and besides, those people were always in trouble.

Carnahan attached the prosthesis that substituted for the lower half of his right leg – a sacrifice he had made to the tough streets of Cincinnati. He dressed quickly in jeans and a short-sleeved uniform shirt, a soiled one from earlier that day, then pulled on the old boots he wore when he fished the river.

He reckoned they would be looking for signs of life, calling out, hoping for a reply. Ninety-nine times out of a hundred kids either got lost or got into something they shouldn't and just didn't go home for a while. They usually weren't hard to find and turned out to be all right. *This is not the kind of thing Tellis would call me for except…* Deep inside he worried this was the hundredth case. *Something in Paul's voice…damn!*

Matthew and Rebecca had ridden with Otis Caslow back to his place, where he made the call to Sheriff Tellis. The three of them and Corly had tramped a few hundred feet up and down stream from Patton's trailer, calling out the boys' names, praying they were within hearing. Rebecca had agreed to try again, hoping against hope that together they might succeed where she alone had given up. Once, Otis thought he detected a child's cry. Whatever he had heard did not repeat, however, and the flurry of anticipation died as quickly as it had been born. Finally, they agreed to call the law.

Paul Tellis at first tried to talk them out of what he perceived was an overreaction. He had been working late in the office and took the call instead of the deputy on duty, who had been handling some other complaint.

"They probably walked farther than they were used to or they're just trying to act like big boys. I pushed my folks pretty hard when I was a little fellow like Billy Joe."

Otis said little as he listened to the remote voice: "Yes" when he tended to agree and "No" when in doubt, signaling to his wife and the anxious parents the mood of the dialogue. Rebecca inched closer to the receiver at Otis's ear, tilting her head to hear for herself the sheriff's words.

"Thank you, Sheriff. But this isn't like Billy Joe. And little Junie isn't but four. There's nothing good we can think of for them being out this late. Appreciate you coming over right away, because Matthew and me are getting ready to go back by the water and start looking again whether you come or not."

"Be by in a few minutes!" Tellis hung up abruptly. He tried to mask his exasperation, but a mixture of politics, duty and genuine concern moved him to call Stubby Carnahan and log out with the duty deputy.

Otis frowned at the Sheriff's reluctance and paced impatiently, troubled by his growing fears. Rebecca stood dumbly by, rocking slowly on her heels, wrapped in self embrace, all but certain that no good would come of this night.

Matthew, Rebecca and Otis waited outdoors about twenty minutes, bathing in perspiration. They adjourned inside the air-conditioned trailer when Sheriff Tellis arrived, then fidgeted another quarter hour for Carnahan. Like sentries on post, the men and Rebecca, despite the growing pain and stiffness from her fall on the road, kept watch, fortified by iced sweet tea Missy poured from a gallon jar.

It was nearly eleven-thirty when Deputy Carnahan pulled onto the gravel driveway that led off the Old State Road into Caslow's place.

Sheriff Tellis had convinced them they needed the experienced hand of the veteran officer, who also brought with him a better searchlight than their C-battery flashlights. Stubby was the best investigator in the Sheriff's Department, a former police detective who one day just showed up and offered his services. A professional law enforcement officer was a relative rarity in the highly politicized realm of the county sheriff, and welcome in the likes of Wheeler County where there were no towns of any size with a truly professional police force.

The Sheriff heard Rebecca out on her fear of Gypsies. He knew they had passed through in June, migrating north with the birds. Except for a rare few stragglers, they would not be by again until fall. They might be thieves and cheats, but they didn't harm children. On the other hand, he paid attention when she told of hearing the dogs. They usually stayed away from humans, but there was no telling what they might do if they were agitated or hungry enough. A feral pack had pulled down some lambs recently; farmers had reported strays prowling around their pastures and yards. And drowning was always a possibility.

The group moved in a three-vehicle caravan back to the home place. Tellis persuaded Rebecca and Missy to stand by the phone at the Millington cottage, on the chance someone might find the lost boys and call. He did not want the women along on the search. Rebecca reluctantly agreed. If the boys were on the road, they might be seen by passersby. Corly went to be with her girls and hide as best she could from reality.

Before setting out, Tellis questioned Matthew, seeking any useful insight on the boys' whereabouts, adding to the general information he had already gathered. He acknowledged the man's distress and attempted to put him at ease.

"Which way did they go from the house?"

"I didn't much notice; just toward the water."

"Did they carry off anything besides their poles?"

"No. But I give 'em store cookies to put in their pockets. And I give Billy Joe some headcheese for bait. Sometimes crappie'll take anything you put on a hook. Depends."

"How were they dressed, Patton?" Tellis's voice took on a harder edge as Matthew digressed.

"Short pants, I guess. Barefoot, maybe. Flip-flops? Awful hot. And they wasn't goin' far I didn't think. I don't know. I'm not for sure. You know what I mean?"

"When's the last time you saw them?"

"About six-thirty. Corly and the girls gone to the Wal-Mart."

"...and you were doing what? Where were you?"

"I was out back fixin' my truck; it don't run too good."

"And you didn't see or hear them any more?"

14

"No, sir! Not a peep!"

"So, as far as you know, they went off to fish in the river?" A hint of contempt crept into the Sheriff's voice. The man's irresponsibility grated on him.

Matthew nodded vaguely and stared off into the darkness after the questioning ended, as if in a trance. A pained expression spread across his dust-turned-to-mud-stained face. He lifted a cigarette to his lips, inhaled deeply, then let out a thick cloud that flowed blue in the halogen headlamps. His head shook slowly from side to side. He wanted no part of this.

Rebecca tearfully confirmed that her son had worn blue shorts, flip-flops, and a new white and red striped T-shirt.

Sheriff Tellis explained his search plan, satisfied he had taken all the time he could justify. The four men would fan out from the riverbank starting from Patton's trailer, to the line of scrub and trees and occasional wire fence that generally marked the back yards – such as they were – and fields, then move downriver toward The Point. The Sheriff concluded, as Rebecca had earlier, that was the most likely place the boys would go to fish. The going would be slow and tedious. The uneven scrubby terrain, oddly placed dwellings and clutter of wrecked cars, dumped home appliances and debris compounded the difficulties of searching at night. Everything was a potential hazard or hiding place. Stubby would take the bank – he knew how to probe the undergrowth – Caslow next to him, then Patton. Tellis would anchor the left, coordinate and take on the responsibility of looking into the yards and out by the road when he had a clear line of sight. He called his dispatcher to send a car to look along the road and told him about the search plan. He and Carnahan carried walkie-talkies.

If nothing turned up, he would need a more intensive and expanded effort in the morning: more men, tracking dogs, and a crew to drag the river – the State Police. He prayed they would find the children unharmed. His efforts needed to be neither too little in case of a real tragedy, nor too much, if they had already turned up. He was willing to risk the ridicule of taking so seriously two little Tacker brats coming home late from fishing in the river.

"Now, Caslow, Patton, you watch me and Stubby, stay even, look over at one of us every few minutes. It's pretty dark and rough out there, so just shine your lights and look a few yards ahead of you at the ground, then from side to side. Move the beam in bands about two or three yards wide. If there's anything there, you'll see it. And don't be afraid to make noise, we want those young ones to hear us. You got any questions?" He spoke as from a textbook to children learning by rote.

"What if we see something?" Otis said.

"Just stop and holler out. We'll come to you. OK?"

Caslow nodded assent and Matthew shrugged his shoulders, resigned to the ordeal ahead. The deputy just looked knowingly at his boss and turned to his right, facing the direction of the search. He walked steadily despite his artificial leg, and could keep pace with most men.

"Let's get going," Tellis said, taking the lead.

They moved out, slowly, cautiously, calling the boys' names as they went. The river flowed past them and melted into the moonless night. Not a raccoon, possum or even a house cat stirred. Only the sounds of their breaking trail, the chirruping of insects and frogs, and from time to time the splash of a fish breaking the water's surface interrupted the silence.

 The party had been searching for more than a half hour when they approached The Point. Tellis had paced them to the slowest man, predictably Matthew Patton, who still lagged several yards behind.

"Hey, hey! Over here! I think I found something! Careful where you put your feet!"

At Carnahan's shout, Tellis closed from the left, overtaking Caslow and reaching the shallow depression where his deputy stood, about ten feet from where the bank jutted into the river. The wide arc of the deputy's light focused on a pair of boy's cotton short pants.

"Damn," Tellis said just under his breath. He thought of the cases of wanton sexual molestation with which the news and law enforcement bulletins were filled. Until this moment, he had not considered that possibility.

Matthew and Otis panicked. They stared into the illuminated circle, bent over and reached out their hands.

"Don't touch 'em! Stand right where you are until I say you can move!"

The men froze at the authority of the sheriff's voice. They straightened slowly, their hearts pounding.

Stubby Carnahan leaned close to examine the pants under the high intensity lamp; they were a faded blue. With a ballpoint pen he lifted a corner where the label lay hidden. "Size 4." He said softly to the Sheriff, who stood inches away across the circle of light, "Could be the Millington boy's. No blood. That's good. But they're damp, smells like urine...and there's feces."

He inspected the ground closely within a seven or eight foot radius. "Something else." A clump of wild growth near the river's edge half-concealed another garment. "Looks like underpants." He read the label aloud. "Hanes, 4."

Matthew Patton let out a wail. He staggered around the site blindly then stumbled and fell in a heap. Otis Caslow and Sheriff Tellis lifted him and rested him sitting with his back against the wide trunk of a red oak tree.

Patton grabbed at the Sheriff's shirt. "They's all right! Those boys is all right! Lord, they's all right, ain't they?" He was not fit to go on.

Poor sonofabitch! Tellis's disdain was turning to compassion. *He's half crazy. Lordy, I wouldn't want to live with what he's feeling right now.*

The Sheriff said to Carnahan, "Better just leave him be for awhile. I got a real bad feeling, Stub. Pick those up and mark where you found 'em. If we got to, we can take pictures in the morning. If…well, I just think we need to be real careful about now." His voice faded to a hoarse whisper as dire scenes played inside his head.

Carnahan picked up the stained underpants. He had no evidence kit, so he held them and the shorts gingerly in one hand, away from his body. He carefully marked the spots where the clothing had lain, using scraps of paper from his pocket, pinned with sharp twigs. He looked carefully for visible evidence of animal or human tracks on the dry ground. There were signs of disturbance, but the men's trampling, especially Patton's lurching delirium, had spoiled what might already have been there. Daylight and a crime scene investigation team would disclose more.

"Caslow, you stay here with Patton!" Tellis said. He lowered his voice to Carnahan. "I don't want Patton around when – if – we find something awful happened." He turned back to the two civilians. "And don't neither of you two walk down this way unless we call you. If we don't find those young ones tonight, we got to look for signs when it gets light. Understand?" He spoke consolingly but with absolute authority. He was taking things much more seriously now.

The search radiated from the spot where the underpants were found. Matthew huddled by his tree, attended by Otis Caslow, as the other two resumed. Tellis would probe the ground along the yards. The expert Carnahan kept to his track in the scrub that lined the riverbank. It was a bad sign their calls had not been answered. The scarcity of other nocturnal life signs confirmed his fears that feral dogs had recently run through here. His stomach was turning sour as curdled milk.

The sheriff and his deputy advanced by inches behind fluttering fans of light. Their track took them deeper into The Point, a sprawl of tangled growth. Carnahan slowed, played his beam through the clutter and moved to his right, favoring his bad leg, into the bight of land where the river bent

18

away. Sheriff Tellis widened his zone away from the river and began to think he needed to wait for daylight and more manpower.

"Oh, God! My God!"

Tellis scrambled toward Carnahan's cry. The radio hissed. He heard a muted "Paul...here...," followed by the sound of retching.

CHAPTER THREE

Two child-sized white coffins sat side-by-side on dark stained wooden stands in a parlor of the Jones-Purdy-Maclamore funeral home. The lids were closed. A simply framed photograph was propped at the head of each, the image of a little boy in life. The troubled living milled about the plain boxes, contemplating the terrible deaths of the little boys.

The Medical Examiner had released Billy Ray's and Junie's bodies to the parents late Thursday and had them taken by hearse to the mortuary to be prepared for burial. Mortician Glenn Purdy had overseen more pleasant tasks. Visitation was limited to Friday afternoon and evening. At the urging of Brother Dewey Cadwell, pastor of the Bethel Church, the families had agreed to hold the funeral and burial at ten o'clock the next morning.

Only a few people had come to pay their respects, mostly from Tackbottom and the church. Pastor Cadwell and his wife had been and gone and would return soon to continue ministering to the bereft parents. The parlor-sized room was about half filled. An expected crowd of the morbidly curious did not materialize, to the relief of Sheriff Paul Tellis, who stood by his car in the parking lot. Tellis took in the scene with pokerfaced detachment. Television crews from two Lexington network affiliate stations, an Associated Press stringer, and reporters from the Lexington Herald-Leader and the Louisville Courier-Journal gathered in the shade of mature oaks and beeches that lined the sidewalk and ornamented the front lawn. They questioned anyone who would speak with them, whether knowledgeable or not. They had been denied access to the small chapel, but they would get their stories.

"These vultures are here because they think two little kids from The Bottoms went fishing and got mauled by wild dogs," Tellis said to Deputy Wendell Murchin, who stood close by his boss.

"I can hear it now: 'Incompetent Sheriff! Screwed up county government! Need stronger animal control laws!' Maybe jump on poor old Patton for neglecting the kids. They'll milk their stories, put them away, then dust them off next time something goes wrong. Wait'll they find out what we think really happened."

Tellis's cynicism about the media yielded to deeper, more troubling thoughts. He exchanged pleasantries with the reporters he knew - a political necessity - but kept a practiced and anxious eye out for others who might show up. Someone who would have no obvious reason to come – not a neighbor, relative, public official – someone who just didn't look right. Violent force had been applied to the little boys' fragile bodies by someone or something besides the wild dogs. The State Police laboratory was following up on evidence gleaned from the scene, but the case rested squarely within the County Sheriff's jurisdiction and under his responsibility.

Inside, Deputy Dale Carnahan stood back in the parlor to one side, opposite where the families of the two little boys clustered, consoling and being consoled. The numbing pain of loss and the exhaustion of sleeplessness hung on them like chains.

Carnahan had found the mutilated bodies. He was also the designated primary investigating officer, a duty that would become increasingly personal. He studied the family members and the sparse crowd with professional disinterest. Not quite sure what he was looking for, he did not want to give the impression that he was conducting an investigation. He fingered the end of the dark brown uniform tie he rarely wore. The deputy thrived in the field, working a case, the vestige of his years as a police detective. Rarely had he an occasion to test his skills since coming to this tiny Kentucky county in the foothills of Appalachia. Maybe this would be one of those times.

Two chattering women near the front batted the humid air with paper fans furnished by the funeral home. The air conditioning worked, but not well. The heat of July 1995 had carried over into August; the temperature outside would reach nearly ninety-five degrees by four. Odors of perspiring bodies, some disguised by sweet smelling toilet water, mingled with the sickly fragrance of wilting flowers and the faint scent of chemicals. Afternoon sunlight streamed through the ceiling-high windows infusing the room with a golden aura.

Up front, Otis and Missy Caslow wept silently. Missy held tightly to her husband's right arm with both hands, her wet face buried in the hollow of his shoulder. Otis's coarse features, ruddy and scored as a cedar log, contorted in grief. He anchored his bulk in front of the coffins, a bulwark against harm set in place too late. Otis had witnessed the finding of the bodies and knew what lay out of view. He believed then and now he could have saved the boys, could have found them, protected them, if Matthew or Rebecca had just come to him sooner.

Otis wheeled and guided his wife to where their sorrowing neighbors waited. He could find no words, no gestures except a slow shake of his head, an affirmation of their loss and their helplessness. Missy threw her arms around Rebecca, who embraced her in return. Their sobs composed a sorrowful duet that drew cascades from the eyes of many in the room.

"My baby! I lost my baby! He's with his daddy and his Pappaw in heaven!" Rebecca emitted a pitiful wail, muffled by a tissue wadded tightly in her hand. It was a wonder she had tears or a voice left. She had gone with her sister-in-law Corly to the hospital where what was left of her son and her nephew had been taken. Matthew had refused to go, disappearing into his twisted little world of denial. Doctor Eddie Khalil had given her some pills after she collapsed. He was director of the Health Clinic and came over as soon as Paul Tellis called. Those pills were all that kept her going.

Corly Patton, dull and glassy-eyed, raised a timid hand to touch Missy's hair. Her pale skin was splotched with red. She acknowledged Missy and Otis with a perfunctory "Thank y'all." "Yes, she said, "they was good little boys. I know they're with Jesus."

Corly had not yet absorbed what had happened. She sought comfort in her girls and shunned other company. It was hard for her to call these people friends and no blood kin of hers were there to share her grief.

Matthew stood away; his coal black eyes were dry, rimmed in crimson. The gaunt face was a granite mask; the bloodless line of his mouth was fixed, defiant. He shifted uneasily on his feet, maintaining distance between himself and the others. He looked past the Caslows at the coffins and spoke aloud to no one and everyone in his pitchman's cant. "Them boys is fishin'. They's out there by the river waitin' for me to fetch 'em home. Ain't Billy Joe and Junie in them pine boxes. Ain't them at all. You know. Ain't our little boys in there. Be goin' down by the river to fetch 'em soon's we leave here." He turned toward Otis. "You know, Otis? You know what I mean?"

Jessie and Annie, the Patton sisters, clung pale and mewling as nursing puppies to their mother. Plainly dressed, lean as their father, the little girls seemed at once older and younger than their six and five years. Their wide brown eyes drifted to the white boxes from time to time. Carnahan marked the shyness and a weariness that mirrored their mother's. Annie, the younger girl, slipped to Rebecca's side, pressed her face into the soft flesh of her aunt's flank, and wiped her nose in the folds of the thin cotton dress.

Pearl Patton fidgeted in her chair, uncomprehending, mumbling inanely about a piece of lace she once sewed to the bodice of a black dress her Momma gave her and wondering aloud why all these people had come to visit when Poppa wasn't at home to greet them properly.

Carnahan waited two or three minutes after the scene had played out and the Caslows had gone. Hat in hand, he marched stiffly down the side aisle, past the yawning rows of worn folding chairs.

He had intended to pass in front of the caskets without stopping, to pay his respects to Matthew and Corly, Rebecca, and old Mrs. Patton, whom he had not met before. Turning to cross the room, he glanced at the photographs of two healthy, smiling children. He stopped between the two tables, not to pray, but to stare, first at one image, then the other. He studied each as he would a crime scene, absorbed the whole and catalogued its parts. His policeman's sense would pick the gold from the dross.

Billy Joe Patton's five by seven inch color portrait showed him thin but hardy, favoring his father. The boy's large head perched atop a birdlike neck; the face was handsome beneath a mass of slicked back hair, black as a crow's wing. The thin mouth turned up slightly in a close-lipped, childish grin, with a hint of defiance. A pale scar on one high cheekbone stood out like a badge of honor against the olive skin. The hollow-set eyes, blue like his mother's, peered from the flat paper, deep with their own secrets like the waters of the river. For eight years old he appeared confident, mature, knowing. He wore a clean, pressed, blue and white plaid cotton shirt. The background, a cloudy blue-gray studio drop, revealed nothing. *Where in this image is the hand that killed him? Who could catch him in his element, the river and its banks, and snuff him? What did those eyes see? Did that mouth cry out?*

And Junie – James Millington, Jr. – a fair-haired doll of a child wearing a short sleeve white dress shirt – sat like a little man at a low wooden table draped in white crepe paper. His bony elbows leaned on the top; tiny hands were curled under his chin. He had his mother's round face and rosy cheeks, her dark Patton eyes.

Four candles burned on the surface of a white iced birthday cake trimmed with blue sugar rosettes. A gel-glazed Ninja Turtles cutout lay between the candles; "Junie" was written in smooth script below them. The little boy goggled in delight. Other children stood in the background, their bodies cropped by the camera's downward angle, focused on the birthday boy. The hems of little dresses, pant legs, socks and shoes showed, surely including those of his Patton cousins. Carnahan took this in within the space of two or three minutes, time that hung as heavy as the questions he could not yet answer. The little boys' photographs took their places in his memory, alongside the indelible images of their mutilated bodies. He shifted his attention to the grieving survivors.

CHAPTER FOUR

Paul Tellis was the reluctant object of a scathing Saturday morning visit from County Judge/Executive Joe Beeler.

"Dammit, Paul, if there's something going on, you need to tell me about it! A half dozen people already told me you're looking for people instead of dogs."

The county's highest elected official hovered over the Sheriff and flapped his arms like a fat, angry buzzard. Sweat seeped down his forehead from under a cheap black toupee, colored to match the dyed remnants of his natural hair.

The Sheriff leaned back in his chair and tried with little success to gain distance from the maw that blasted him from inches away.

Beeler barely controlled himself. As a public official and powerful political figure in his own right, he expected to know everything that happened in his bailiwick.

Tellis smirked into the froggy eyes and flushed face of his long-time rival. Kentucky's system of local government encouraged the creation of competing fiefdoms and nurtured the growth of political dynasties that often played musical chairs with elected offices. The County Judge/Executive, the Sheriff and the County Attorney, the county's civil attorney and prosecutor of misdemeanor crimes, all were county officials, independently elected and not subject to the jurisdiction of the others. The Commonwealth's Attorney, also an elected official, represented the state and was independent of all county officials.

"Now, Joe." Tellis said amid incoming bursts of coffee- and tobacco-laced breath, putting a cheerful edge on his voice. "Now, Joe, why don't you just set your fat ass over there and calm down! You've got no call barging in here, disturbing the peace..."

He paused as Beeler tensed and wiped an already saturated pocket-handkerchief across his face. The sheriff's face broadened into an almost congenial smile, "...well, my peace, anyway."

The Judge/Executive pulled a beat-up wooden armchair to the side of the desk, perched on the edge of the seat and thrust his head forward conspiratorially. He knew to let up if he wanted a constructive answer.

"You know something about who killed those Tacker kids?"

Law enforcement communications and the news generally had been full of child molestation and ritual murder reports. Nothing like that had ever occurred in Wheeler County, but neither had it happened before in many other communities. It was a time when motive could be no more than the thrill of torture or killing. Traditional assumptions went out the window.

The Sheriff's office had reported only that two little boys were found dead in Tackbottom and were presumed killed by a pack of stray dogs that had been terrorizing livestock and farmyards south of Parkersburg. In the wake of that announcement public officials, local citizens and the news media screamed for quick action to catch and destroy the dogs. Many took the Sheriff to task for letting the pack roam uncontrolled for so long, though he was not directly responsible. Under ordinary circumstances, Tellis would have worried about the political consequences of this apparent dereliction. He knew that release of what actually happened would raise to a new level the clamor to find human perpetrators, which was his responsibility.

Tellis, Carnahan and three other deputies had combed The Point with the help of a state crime scene team. Carnahan had speculated that the little boys' bodies may have been intentionally hidden in the underbrush before the dogs got to them. Preliminary autopsy results showed the Millington child might still have been alive. He had been struck in the side of the head by a blunt object that may or may not have been the cause of death. Sharp teeth had gnawed on the children's tender flesh and torn away parts of their bodies, including the smaller boy's genital and rectal areas. Sheriff Tellis thought maybe the dogs were after the lunchmeat and cookies the boys carried with them. Some of Junie Millington's clothing apparently had been removed before he died. His shorts and underpants had been soiled with his urine and feces. Although they would await forensic confirmation, what at first had seemed a tragic incident had turned into a probable double homicide with sickening overtones.

As discreetly as was possible, the Sheriff's people inquired into broader matters under the cover of trying to locate the wild dogs. Some minor thefts of farm property had occurred coincidentally over the past several days in the same general area. Deputies went door to door along the road, into bordering businesses, to delivery services and truckers who may have passed through between Saturday morning and Monday night. Had anyone seen unusual activity along a three- or four-mile stretch having The Point as its approximate midpoint: a vehicle, a stranger? A few of those interrogated asked their own questions in turn, connecting a human hand to the little boys' deaths.

Rumors of a cover-up had risen to the level of gospel by Wednesday evening, and Tellis had restricted all public comment to himself. He stonewalled. He knew that the physical evidence gathered at the death scene pointed to one or more persons having been in the area sometime on Monday. But he had nothing else and he needed time. He also knew well that each day lessened his chances of finding a perpetrator, especially someone not from Wheeler County.

Tellis did not tell Judge Beeler that at that moment Carnahan and another deputy, Wendell Murchin, were speaking with a farmer in South Wheeler, about five miles south of the Interstate. The man had called the previous night, but the Sheriff had spoken with him just an hour ago. He had hauled some produce into town on Monday afternoon and had driven back the Old State Road at about seven thirty or eight in the evening. He had seen a red convertible parked in the grass where the road curved near The Point. It caught his eye because such cars were rare thereabouts.

"Sir, are you sure about the color and that it was a convertible? Did you see what make?

"It were a little car. Looked like a Chevy or Pontiac. Top was down. Kinda new lookin'."

"How about the license plate, do you remember anything about it? What color, was it a Kentucky plate?"

"Well, I believe it were, white with dark numbers, but I didn't pay much attention. It were on the side of the road, facin' toward town. Off in the grass. But I didn't see nobody by the car."

Carnahan entered the answers in his notebook; Murchin wrote a narrative, as well. Burrell Smith, a forty-seven year-old truck farmer, had supplied the first break. He wasn't able to tell them much more, but this information could lead them to something solid.

The three men stood outside the shed where tractors and implements were stored. The sun baked the cleared ground around them. Carnahan had the witness sketch the road and the vehicle's location on a clean sheet of unlined paper. Sweat dripped from the farmer's face onto the page as he leaned across the cruiser's hood and crudely illustrated what he had seen.

Back in the car, Carnahan ordered a search for the red convertible fairly new, likely a 1993 or 1994 model. He asked for the Sheriff, who, he was informed, was "in a meeting" with Judge Beeler. Stubby grinned. Such "meetings" were legendary and usually involved a lot more puffing than public business. Those two men were like roosters who shared the same barnyard – always sparring and occasionally drawing blood.

"Interrupt him, Betty. He'll want to talk to me but you better not say who it is or what this is about in front of 'Old Rottentop'."

Elizabeth Kearney, the duty dispatcher, chuckled into her headset, "You know Joe hates that name; he'd skin you if he heard you say that."

She realized what she had said just as Carnahan's laughter boomed into her ear. The unflattering nickname memorialized Joe Beeler's purchase of a hairpiece that resembled an animal's pelt and his fondness for playing "Rocky Top" on the banjo. Liz Kearney blushed and switched to the intercom.

"Maybe," Carnahan said to his partner as he waited for the connection with their boss, "maybe, we'll get lucky and this is somebody local. Maybe a couple of teenagers making out. Or somebody who saw something else. We'd better get over there and look for tire tracks. Wouldn't be many cars pulled off right there, but it has been nearly a week. Like I said, maybe we'll get lucky."

"Yeah, Stubby, but not as lucky as those teenagers." A grinning Murchin tapped the steering wheel rim to the beat of "Achy Breaky Heart" on the radio as he waited for a line of traffic to pass, then turned north onto the Old State Road. Carnahan's thoughts turned to the events then transpiring in the

Bethel churchyard, where a quiet burial ceremony was underway. He wanted to be there but understood why he was not.

Sheriff Tellis had detailed a deputy not involved in the investigation to attend, primarily to handle traffic and show the face of the Sheriff's office. The deputy knew little about the case and couldn't inadvertently divulge much if asked questions. At least Tellis hoped that would be the case. He also believed that ignorance could be a powerful motivator to meddle. Those who knew the least often said the most just to appear on the inside of what was going on. He would just have to take his chances.

"What you got, Stub?" The Sheriff's voice crackled from the speaker. "I just sent Beeler back to his office, but I had to promise to share with him later today. You know how that burns my ass, but the lid's about to come off anyways."

The deputy broke from his reverie. "I know, Chief," he said. "Well, it isn't much, but we're on our way to look for tire tracks and I called in a color and type on the car. Maybe somebody saw something. We'll let you know."

"Okay. You boys get all the help you need. There's gonna be hell to pay tomorrow when the TV and the papers let out it wasn't dogs that did those kids in. Patty Dennis from over at the *Democrat* has been camped in the lobby all morning. She saw Joe come in and followed him down to his office when he left. I got all kinds of phone calls I won't return today. I can put things off at least one more day."

"We'll do the best we can. I'll gig the state boys for the lab stuff."

Deputy Murchin pulled the car off the road ten or fifteen yards short of where Smith had told them he saw the red convertible. They covered a distance about fifteen feet into the fringe, each taking a position about midway in a ten-foot swath, then slowly walked north, carefully parting the dry field grasses in their path.

"Hey, Stubby, this here looks like something." Murchison flagged with his right arm and pointed with the other hand where the parched ground cover had been pressed down and had only partially recovered.

Both men bent to look closely at parallel lines of tire tracks in the dust.

"No, Murch, these belong to a tractor. Look at those cleat marks, and see, there's a big set and a little one. They go over to that fence line. Let's keep looking." Murchison was green but enthusiastic and Carnahan was a patient and thoughtful teacher.

About twenty feet farther along, the junior deputy called out again, this time after carefully inspecting the ground. "These are a car's."

They stood in a graded area near a culvert that drained under the road. A car had pulled off the asphalt and made a U-turn. Carnahan checked the farmer's sketch. It was close, but the culvert didn't show. "It could be nothing," he said, "but then, we don't have much else right now. Bring me the camera and the plaster kit from the cruiser. Let's play detective."

Carnahan decided not to bother the state forensics people with this. He looked up at the sky. It was close to noon. He glanced at his watch to confirm. Clouds were forming above Old Judge but no rain was forecast to break the dry spell.

The two deputies had returned to the courthouse and were writing up the day's activities when the intercom buzzed. "Stub, can you come up here and see me right away?" Sheriff Tellis said. "One of the boys thinks he knows something about that little red car."

CHAPTER FIVE

Dr. Adib "Eddie" Khalil watched the skies take on a grimy cast through the smudged windows of his office in the County Medical Clinic. The day had been long and full, a Saturday of seeing indigent and Medicaid patients. He needed only to complete some dictation and unwind before going home. His mind wandered to the small hours of Tuesday, when he had been called to meet the Sheriff at the Regional Hospital to examine the mutilated corpses of two young boys who had apparently been killed and devoured by a pack of wild dogs. He had gone with Tellis and the boys' mothers back to his clinic after the bodies had been identified. The remains had then been driven to Lexington for autopsy by the state Medical Examiner's office.

No matter how long he would practice medicine, nothing could prepare him for such a sight. He prescribed the women sedatives, enough to tide them over the next few days. He did not know what to make of his being called. Billy Ray Patton and little James Millington, Jr. had been his patients. He had treated members of their families. The Sheriff, however, like most of the better off residents of the county, avoided his office. Perhaps the women had asked for him. Maybe the Sheriff didn't want to bother any of the other physicians and didn't know who would be on duty at the hospital.

Eddie Khalil emigrated from Palestine, which meant his medical colleagues were free to call him "Towel Head" and "Camel Jockey," demeaning names given to darker-skinned people from South Asia and the Middle East. It made no difference to them that he was a skilled and caring physician or that had married into one of the county's oldest and richest families. Jeannie Ann Dowd was a hellion, anyway, a hippie who went back East to a liberal university. She returned home in June of 1978, at the end of her junior year, three months' pregnant, dragging along an immigrant medical resident from Georgetown University Hospital.

The wedding was quick and quiet and the couple left immediately for Washington, D.C. and the remainder of the groom's residency. Jasper Dowd had not been pleased. Much of his life had been plagued by the rebellion of his youngest child. Paternal indulgence usually overcame the storms of anger loosed by some audacious deed or the accumulation of minor offenses. Peace came, however, at ever-greater cost to the relationship. It was to remedy those effects that a reconciled daughter, her husband and child moved to the family horse farm, an estate built over three generations. Jeannie Ann's older brother, Jasper Payne Dowd, Jr., "Jock," carried on the tradition of Dowd & Dowd, the family law firm. The elder Jasper had reluctantly retired from the practice the previous year.

The intercom's buzzer broke the physician's reverie. Nurse Margaret Ezell said through the speaker, "Dr. K, Jeannie Ann's on line 2. She's kind of upset."

"Thank you, Margaret." He picked up. "Yes, Honey, what's wrong?"

"Eddie, I don't know what's going on! A sheriff's deputy is out here asking about the convertible and who drove it last Monday. I think Joseph might have taken the car while we were out after supper. I didn't want to say

34

anything unless you were here. I started to call Daddy but he'd probably hurt more than help. You need to come home right away!"

He let her finish. It was not in him to interrupt his high-spirited wife of seventeen years.

"Which deputy, Jeannie Ann? What's his name – please? Where is he now?" He used his best bedside voice: low, steady, under control. His speech carried traces of his native Arabic: gently rolled R's and the tendency to sound P's as B's.

"Carnahan. The one that used to be a Cincinnati cop. He says the red car was seen near where those two little Tackbottom boys were found."

"Okay, Darling, put him on the phone and don't you or Joseph say anything until I get there."

"Hi, Dr. K. Look, this is just a follow-up," Carnahan said. "We're trying to find out if whoever was in that car saw anything Monday. You know, the little boys, the dog pack, anybody who could've seen anything. A farmer saw a car that looked like your Pontiac convertible on the County Road near The Point at around seven thirty." Carnahan said just enough to be truthful but not so much that he might reveal his suspicions.

The image of those innocent, mutilated little bodies flashed anew in the physician's mind.

"Of course, Dale." He was intentionally familiar. "Please wait there. I'm leaving now."

Deputies Carnahan and Murchin circled the red Sunbird like hawks above prey. Jeannie Ann and Joseph waited in the screened breezeway between the house and the garage, engaged in animated conversation.

"But Mom, I don't know anything about this. You know Dad told me not to take the car out until it was fixed." The boy looked down into his mother's eyes and spoke rapidly; he hunched his shoulders and held his hands out to her, palms up. Joseph had his father's olive skin and wiry black hair. He stood over six feet two, tall for his sixteen and a half years. In that respect, he favored the Dowds. His social awkwardness, coupled with an exceptionally high IQ, set him up to be bullied by classmates. When he reached the ninth grade his parents had sent him away to boarding school.

Jeannie Ann nodded, glaring between narrowed lids into bottomless black wells, another legacy of his father's line. Despite her own youthful rebelliousness, she abided none of it in her only child – and she believed he was not telling her the truth. "Joseph, you need to talk to me straight. This could be serious." She pressed it no further; she had spotted her father from the corner of an eye. He was striding across the wide, well-kept lawn that separated her comfortable home from the "Big House," where he rattled about in awkward semi-retirement, making do with a much reduced domain but zealous in its rule.

Jasper Dowd skirted the covered porch and made straight for the deputies. He was a large man, nearly six feet, five inches tall, his bulk turning from muscle to fat, but robust at seventy-three.

"Hey, Carnahan!" he said while still several feet away and closing fast. His meaty right hand was extended at the end of a still-powerful arm. "What're you boys doing out here? Did my sawbones son-in-law leave a sponge in somebody?" He exuded a hearty good humor that was both genuine and purposeful.

"Good afternoon, Judge Dowd." Stubby greeted the old man, touched the brim of his trooper-style hat with his fingertips, and reached to shake hands. Jasper Dowd had earned the title not from judicial office but from a local custom that accorded respect to senior attorneys. "No, sir, we're just tracking down a lead that a car resembling this one was seen near Tackbottom the other day about the time those two little boys died. We think that whoever was in it might help us figure out what happened. Maybe saw the dogs or the little boys walking near the road."

36

The old lawyer held the other man's hand in a cordial but insistent grip and locked his gaze on the deputy's tanned, professionally inscrutable face. His instincts, fed by years of experience reading people and ferreting out truth, warned him that something more was going on. The deputy's handshake was a little too hearty, the features too composed, the voice a shade too earnest.

"Well, looky there!" Dowd motioned toward the road with his left hand, at the same time releasing his hold with the right. "Here comes the quack himself. You can ask him about it."

Joseph and his mother stepped out from under the breezeway when the Buick sedan turned in from the road. The deputies approached Dr. Khalil as he got out of the car, but he bypassed them and his father-in-law and went straight to his wife and son. He led them under the eaves of the house, where they held a brief, whispered conversation. That done, the father moved toward the others.

After obligatory pleasantries were exchanged, Carnahan came to the point, politely but with purpose.

"Sir, we can save a lot of time if we could just know whether anybody was driving this car last Monday over by Tackbottom. We're just trying to find witnesses. Nobody is a suspect...I mean, we don't know what happened. We're just trying to do our jobs. The sooner we eliminate possibilities the sooner we can close the case."

The slip was not lost on the doctor or on his father-in-law, casting doubt on the public line and supporting rumors that a human hand, not feral dogs, had slain the boys.

Carnahan flicked frequent glances at Joseph and his mother standing back in the shadows. They appeared cool and disinterested, but the mother's stance, like a lioness shielding her cub, caught his attention.

Jasper Dowd said, "Hell, Eddie, if this is the car somebody saw, you should say so. If it is, it's innocent enough that you or the boy – he had eliminated his daughter from suspicion – were just over there for whatever reason." His tone was overly sincere, almost baiting. It was part of his perverseness that he could adore his youngest child and at the same time feel contempt for her husband and their son, his flesh and blood.

Eddie Khalil wavered. He had elicited from Joseph that the boy had indeed taken the car against orders and had broken down on the road near The Point. He believed his son had not had a hand in anything this horrible but part of him distrusted the law enforcement officers, and his wife's father, as well. Reluctantly, he agreed to let his son be questioned, so long as he, Jeannie Ann and Jasper were present. Joseph clung to his mother's hand.

"No, I was not there." The boy's answer to the deputy's first question drew looks of disbelief from his parents.

Carnahan noted their reactions and pressed on. "Now, Joseph – is it okay if I call you Joseph?" Receiving a shoulder shrug in reply, he continued. "A car like this was seen parked off the road in Tackbottom at about 7:30 Monday evening. Even if you weren't supposed to be there, it's not such a terrible thing if by telling the truth you help us figure out what happened to those two little kids. Now, I'm not saying you had anything to do with it, but if you were there, maybe you saw something, them walking by the road, the dog pack, other people or cars. You know. Help us like you'd want somebody to help if something bad happened to a member of your family."

The boy straightened his back and released his grip on his mother's hand. "All right. So I drove the car when my folks went out. Something is wrong with it. Like, it gets real hot and then stops. It cools off and starts again. That's what happened."

"Did you leave the car?"

"No."

"Did you see anything like I described?"

The boy's mood darkened. "Dad. Mom. I don't want to talk any more. This man scares me, you know. Like, he thinks I've done something wrong. Grandfather, can I stop?"

Jasper Dowd put on his advocate's hat — he sensed that Joseph was hiding something — "Let's call it a day, boys, you can talk to him some more later."

"Okay, Judge Dowd, but we'd like to go ahead and look over the car while we're here. You know I can get a warrant if I need to. We're only doing our jobs. You know that."

With Eddie Khalil's permission, Stubby Carnahan and Wendell Murchin carefully examined the Sunbird convertible. They prepared molds of the tire treads and removed the floor mats from the front seat. They scraped residue from the gas and brake pedals and collected waste fluids from under the engine and transmission.

Their evidence gathering completed, Carnahan addressed Dr. Khalil. "Sir, we probably will want to talk with your son again. If he did see anything, he could be a big help. If it's okay with you, I'll call Monday morning and we can have you bring him down to the courthouse."

The mention of "courthouse" sent a chill through parents and son. Khalil gathered his wife and child in his arms and glared at the backs of the departing officers.

As the cruiser was disappearing down the road, Dowd exploded. He charged at his grandson and barely refrained from manhandling him. "What the hell is going on here? Joseph, why are you lying? Are you into something? Talk to me, you little wimp! Like it or not, you're a Dowd and whatever you do reflects on me! We've been on this land a long time and we'll be here until hell freezes over!"

The old man's thinly disguised contempt burst forth. He had wanted badly to keep peace with his daughter and had gone through the motions for years, but no one doubted his unhappiness. It was to him as if a plow horse had mounted one of his thoroughbred brood mares: both the sire and the offspring dishonored the stable.

"You sad, sorry old man!" Eddie Khalil erupted in his own tirade. "You think you know about the land? That you have a family? How long have the Dowds been here? One hundred years?" Khalil scoffed at the number. "My father's village was founded by Saladin himself eight hundred years ago. You know him? He kicked the Crusaders out of Palestine. I have ten thousand cousins. But for the Jews, we would still have the land! Don't talk to me about family and land!"

Barely twelve inches separated the enraged doctor and his red-faced father in law. Jasper Dowd braced, fists clenched by his sides. He was not used to being challenged, let alone spoken to in such a way. Yet he seemed to be rendered uncharacteristically mute.

Eddie raged on. "You treat me as an outsider. Many of my people in Israel were thrown out after the '48 war but came back. They stay, but they have no rights, no land, no citizenship!"

The old lawyer broke in, sputtered and raised his arms as if to strike. He leaned down almost nose-to-nose and screamed into his son in law's face. "That's no concern of mine you goddamn towel head! You people only got what you deserved!"

There, it was out, words spoken that could never be taken back. Jeannie Ann, already stunned by her husband's tirade, gasped at her father's declaration. She had long tolerated his arrogance, his disdain for those not like him, but never before had he directed it this way.

40

Eddie pressed on, unintimidated. His passion overrode whatever fear of physical harm he may have felt. His words were true and his cause just. There was no backing down.

"You people? You talk about my people and what we deserve? I will never belong here, either, will I? How do I deserve that? And you carry that to your grandson. How does he deserve that? You say you love his mother, but you demean her in many ways. Why? Because she rebelled against you, and Joseph and I are the tangible reminder of her *Intifada*!"

The doctor took a deep breath, his energy waning. He opened the distance between them and jabbed a finger at the taller man's face.

"You may hate me for whatever reason but how can you despise your own blood! If you wish to live with that, so be it, but never again speak to me of land or family. Your words damn you as a fool and a hypocrite!"

Dowd ignored the accusatory finger and final condemnation. At the mention of his daughter, he had shifted his focus to where Jeannie Ann stood, guarding her son. The steel in her eyes validated her husband's attack. Where he expected a daughter's loyalty, he saw only contempt.

His face twisted as much in anguish as with fury, Dowd abruptly turned his back and stalked toward the big house with the purposefulness of a general breaking off a bloody engagement. The lack of rebuttal confounded him as much as it must have astonished his daughter and her husband, both all too familiar with his contentiousness.

Jeannie Ann had listened in disbelief, holding her son suffocatingly close. Where did all this hate come from? What did all of this bode for her? For Joseph?

Joseph was a brilliant and sensitive young man. Jeannie Ann knew he would process what had passed between his father and grandfather and turn it to his own purposes. It was a game his mind played with words, with numbers, with ideas, with simple, everyday events. She shuddered that the dominant qualities he had acquired from her were the practiced ability to build alterative realities and to lie with a straight face.

In her youth Jeannie Ann had fabricated to escape a world she found bigoted and oppressive. Hers was a deception of exaggeration. However onerous the charge, she confessed to a greater sin, aiming to conquer by shock, to numb her judges, most often her parents, who would gratefully accept the actual indiscretion as preferable to the made-up one. The accommodations of marriage, motherhood and a return to her father's grace had damped but not put out the fire that now flared within her. If her son was in trouble, it must be she who would protect him.

Joseph understood immediately what was going on. This was not about him. Absorbed in themselves and their roles, his parents and grandfather had lost sight of the central character in this unfolding crisis. All this fuss and furor were for their benefit, not for his. Jasper Dowd had exposed his revulsion and duplicity to full light. Eddie Khalil's assault was in defense of the father and not of the son. And Jeannie Ann, doting mother, was lost in that complex and contradictory world of self-doubt and self-justification that affirms the dependency of the child and the unending duty of the parent.

The afternoon's tumult both terrified the boy and left him strangely stimulated. He knew in his deepest recesses, if not at the surface of reason, that he did not belong here, in this place, in these circumstances.

Joseph struggled to hold back tears and tore away from his mother's smothering embrace. Like a wounded bear, he lurched into the house and lumbered up the back stairs to his room and sanctuary.

CHAPTER SIX

The irony of her father's claims to an ancient and illustrious ancestry was not lost on Jeannie Ann Dowd. Jasper Dowd traced his line to the same Frankish nobles who conquered the Saxons in 1066 and ruled in the Holy Land in the next century. From Rossignan to Fitzhugh and through centuries of breeding and intermarriage, to the Irish Dowds and emigration to America in the 18th Century, pride of blood and attachment to the land sustained his ancestors through adversity and prosperity. Protestantized over the years, the line converted from the Church of Rome and eventually into the congregation of John Calvin. Jasper Dowd proudly served as an elder in the Presbyterian Church.

The Kentucky Dowds, wealthy and respected, were not far removed from Appalachian poverty and isolation. Whatever the gaps in genealogy, the births out of wedlock, the offsets where the ancestral line did not join straight and true, however, the family held to its traditions, some would say myths, of landed gentry.

Jeannie Ann knew also of her father's attachment to the pseudo-aristocracy of modern Templarism. He had for many years belonged to the Sovereign Military Order of the Temple of Jerusalem, an American incarnation of the Knights Templar, whose announced purpose was to facilitate the growth of the virtues of Christian gentlemen and ladies, Knights and Dames by title. Its principal mission was charity and Jasper Dowd used it as a means to do good works, with the added benefit of contacts with a Christian elite of congressmen, clergy, judges, and generals across the country. Membership reinforced his self-image as the legitimate heir to a noble heritage and counterbalanced the occasional moral and ethical lapses of an affluent lifestyle.

Eddie Khalil's ancestral village, Hattin, had indeed been reestablished by Saladin in 1187, nearly a century after its evacuation in the First Crusade, and was obliterated by the Jews in 1948, leaving only a wall, a ruined mosque and a shrine to the Prophet Jethro.

After Israeli troops drove his family from their home Eddie's father led his pregnant wife and two children to a Lebanese refugee camp.

Milada Khalil, his mother, at first refused to go. "This is our land and our faith!" she said. "If they want to kill me, they will need to shoot me where I stand!"

As Eddie grew in his mother's womb, he absorbed that love of family and home, of the dream of Palestine, of blood, land and heritage – and the reality of diaspora. The mother's passion passed him by, however, to be relit and stoked in her grandson.

Joseph's Saladin fantasy role-play persona arose from a much earlier confrontation between Muslims and western invaders during the Third Crusade, culminating in Saladin's momentous victory over the Crusaders on July 4, 1187, at the Battle of Hattin, Unlike the burly Joseph, his role model was small of stature and frail, but of towering intellect and courage.

The Crusaders had fought from a close formation of mounted knights and infantry armed with pikes and bows, protected against arrows in leather cloaks and mail. The Muslims in their turn had employed intermittent charges of light cavalry and mounted archers, picking away the Christian troops, wearing them down. When the parched and exhausted infantry fled in search of water they left the sluggish knights vulnerable to Saladin's bowmen, who shot their mounts from under them. Pursuing horsemen picked off the fleeing foot soldiers. Thousands were killed or taken prisoner and only a few knights, including some two hundred Knights Templar, survived.

When the battle ended, Saladin received the captives, including their leader, King Guy, in his tent. As his prisoners drank cold water to quench the thirst of their ordeal, Saladin with his own hand first severed an arm then beheaded Prince Renaud de Chatillon, a knight Saladin believed guilty of treachery and blasphemy. He then ordered the Templars executed for the equivalent of war crimes – cruel and wanton taking of Muslim lives in previous military actions. The rest of his captives if not ransomed, as were the King and his train, were sold into slavery. Discretion in applying the customs of war, retribution or desert hospitality belonged solely to the warrior leader, and each decision was justified on its own terms.

Warring continued for five years more, with the Crusaders never recovering fully from their defeat at Hattin. In 1192, King Richard the Lionheart of England and Saladin concluded a truce by whose terms the Christians were permitted to visit Jerusalem with full access to the holy places. The following year Saladin took ill of a fever and lay prostrate for nearly two weeks when, in the company of family and companions, he smiled broadly and breathed his last.

The animosity between the branches of Joseph Khalil's lineage was embedded in his genes. The eight centuries old raw nerve had never healed and was inflamed anew in his father and grandfather. They left him with no clear sense of who he was or where was his place in the world.

CHAPTER SEVEN

The hard little ball slammed into the crotch of the near corner, barely three inches above the glossy boards, and dribbled harmlessly toward the service line. Albert Thornburg grunted as he picked himself off the floor where he had landed in a futile lunge to reach the unreturnable kill shot. "Maxie, you lousy bastard!"

The stocky little man who had just made a perfect shot to win the rubber game turned his face to the side and hid a mischievous grin from his much younger opponent. On a given day, 63-year-old Mario "Maxie" Giuliano could beat the best of his diverse collection of racquetball rivals, and he consistently outthought them. Introduced to handball on his twelfth birthday by a compassionate police sergeant concerned that the chubby lad lacked athletic ability, Maxie had switched to racquetball in the early 1980's when the population of worthy competitors all but disappeared. As time passed, he made up in experience and intelligence what he gradually lost in quickness and agility.

"Why do I let you do that to me, you old fart? You get me into a slow game and then catch me nailed to the back wall." Thornburg smiled broadly as he extended a gloved hand. He found himself nodding his head in reluctant deference, much as a bright, over-confident student might regard a professor whom he respected but considered his intellectual inferior.

Albert Thornburg had met defeat at Maxie's hands before, both on the racquetball court and in criminal trial court. Thornburg was the Jefferson County Commonwealth's Attorney's brightest young assistant prosecutor and Maxie was a legend of the criminal defense bar.

"Come along, my boy, and I'll stand for a double orange juice. Now, what did you learn today?" Maxie's tone was half serious, half mocking. "Keep to the center, Al, and stay low, like I do." He chuckled self-effacingly at the reference to his height - or lack of it; his colleague stood six inches taller at six feet three inches. The man was a natural teacher and it was widely believed that he could have been a successful standup comic had he not chosen to practice law. In his student and early practice years, he stood constantly at the brink of censure - or worse - because of his brutally accurate mimicry of professors and judges.

Freshly showered, impeccably turned out and ready for a full Tuesday afternoon of work, Maxie burst with the enthusiasm of a young bull into the plainly furnished reception area of his modest offices. Despite his professional and financial successes, he retained much of the simplicity and frugality of his youth.

"What's hot, Willie Mae?" Maxie said to his secretary and right arm, Willie Mae Norton.

"You and chili peppers, Mr. G!" With her response she handed him a glass of freshly made vegetable juice. For twenty years, he had greeted her in this way on returning to the twelfth floor of the Jefferson Tower at mid-day. And for twenty years her answer had been the same. Maxie had introduced her to the salutary effects of chili peppers during her first week on the job as an unsuspecting rookie fresh from secretarial school. The youthful Willie Mae was determined not to be intimidated and had taken a healthy swig of her new boss's version of V8 juice loaded with liquid heat. She didn't blink, even as the tongue boiled in her mouth and sweat poured from her forehead.

Maxie paid careful attention to what went into his body. Only he was allowed to dose up the drinks; it had been just five years since he allowed even Willie Mae to prepare the basic juices. The ritual fulfilled, Willie Mae would inform him of any matter urgent enough not to wait for his afternoon rustle through the piles of mail, memos and phone messages.

"Maxie, you need to call Jock Dowd over in Parkersburg. He wants to talk to you about some teenager suspected of killing those two little boys. I think it's his nephew. Anyway, it sounded urgent and he wants you to call him right back."

"Lord, Willie Mae, that case's got warts all over it — mutilation, witchcraft, and Judge Benny Willards. Jock doesn't need me; he needs different relatives."

Maxie had followed the public accounts. The case was circumstantial, but decent, with two of the suspects accusing a third. He knew that Jock Dowd's nephew was the odd man out, a loner; said to be a little weird. It would be a high profile prosecution with all kinds of negatives for the defense.

"Jock, Maxie Giuliano. What's this case about?"

"You sure as hell get right to the nubbin. No 'how's it hangin' or 'will I see you in Lexington next month?'" Jock Dowd's salty joviality and good old boy patter belied his Ivy League education and worldly sophistication.

"Okay, Jock. How's it hanging? How's the easy life over in East Paradise with the Dowd royal family? And why do you need me? Your client's the strange kid?"

"You're right, Maxie, let's get to the point," said Dowd. "Yeah, he's my sister Jeannie Ann's boy. Her husband's Palestinian, a doctor. Runs a clinic here. Senior has been a real bastard, claiming that the kid's no blood of his and driving poor Jeannie Ann wild. She begged me to get Joseph a good lawyer. I'm in the middle on this, but he needs all the help he can get."

"I read some about this in the papers and followed it on the tube. It's been quite a deal, this, and all the publicity about those homicidal teenagers in Arkansas and the two little Brits killing for fun. Just don't know what the hell is getting into these youngsters. Are they going to try the case there? I sure wouldn't want a local jury served up with Benny Willards' home cooking."

"Those are some of the issues. Not only publicity and a political judge, but also the other two kids are star athletes who were going off to college this fall. They're both 18, Joseph's just 16, and it's too early to tell what's going to happen. Their daddies are part of the good old boy network. One's the State Farm agent; other owns a Toyota dealership. Eddie Khalil, Jeannie Ann's husband, is a competent physician, but he's still an outsider. They sent Joseph off to boarding school because he had such a hard time getting along here. Brilliant kid, but he just doesn't fit in. Dowd blood doesn't seem to make much difference, either, especially since my father's so hard set against his son-in-law. It's hard to explain, because he really dotes on Jeannie Ann." The longer he talked, the more Jock Dowd's speech smoothed, losing its provincial affectations and country gentleman's drawl.

"When can I come down to see them? I'd rather do it there. I understand the boy's not been charged yet. I'd like to talk to him right away. I'm available Thursday, day after tomorrow. And you can give me all you know or can find out about the case. What's the evidence? Forensics? Who's going to prosecute? Everything about the investigation. I understand a sheriff's deputy has done most of the work." Maxie rattled off his list, staccato, focusing on the components of a defense. It was a sure sign of his visceral interest in the case and where his gut went, Maxie's mind was certain to follow.

"I'll make sure you get everything you need and call you back as soon as I set up the meeting. Thursday sounds doable. Thanks, pardner, I surely do appreciate this. I surely do." Dowd's sign-off expressed not only his gratitude and relief but also betrayed his underlying anxiety.

Maxie drained the glass of carrot-celery juice laced with Louisiana Pepper Sauce then hollered for Willie Mae through the open door. Despite a state-of-the-art intercommunication system, the seasoned barrister preferred old-fashioned acoustics – the unaided, self-amplified voice.

"Yes, Mr. G," Willie Mae said through the speaker on his desk. Maxie's bluster had never daunted her. He had his ways, but she had hers as well. Each tolerated the other with a mutual respect and affection nurtured over the years.

"Get Susan in here!"

Susan Wycov strode into Maxie's office, a laptop computer in one hand and a mug of steaming black coffee in the other. "Hey, Mr. G., did you whip that arrogant asshole Thornburg at noon?" She mischievously parroted Willie Mae's proprietary name for Maxie. "You know, he opposed a continuance the other day on one of your cases just to piss me off because I turned him down for a date. Said if court was the only place he could see me, then we'd just have to spend more time there."

Susan dropped her lanky frame into a worn leather chair beside the desk and leaned forward. She laid the laptop and cup on the bare surface of the mahogany desk, pushed the long straight brown hair away from her face and looked her boss in the eye.

Maxie laughed aloud, his eyes narrowing and fixed on his young associate. He pushed a ceramic coaster towards her and shook his head from side to side, partially in mock disapproval of her unceremonious entry and partially in appreciation of her uninhibited style. Her pose reminded him, somewhat egotistically, of a sunflower angled to receive the sun's light. *Where,* he thought, *does all this energy and eagerness come from?*

He jabbed at her good humoredly. "You've turned down half the young bucks in the bar and a lot of the old bastards who just wanted to get into your pants. One of these days you may just have to make a choice. They don't take JAPs into convents, you know."

"Maxie, you know I'm just waiting for you to make your play. I'll save myself until then."

This brassy, open quality set her off from the "what's in it for me" kids who came looking for a soft ride out of law school. She had finished near the top of her Georgetown Law class and wanted to come back home to Louisville. Despite her excellent credentials, she put off the large law practices. She had outraged the managing partner of the state's largest and most prestigious firm. In response to obtuse questions designed to elicit information he could not directly ask about, she had offered her own paraphrase: "You want to know about my social life, if I sleep around and why I'm not married. If fornication is a prerequisite to practicing here, I'm afraid I'll have to pass. I could never keep up with you guys."

So, she brought her brain and irreverent manner to Maxie Giuliano's door where, for a fraction of the pay she might have commanded, she had for the past two years apprenticed herself to the service of drunks, whores, thieves, addicts and just plain folks who got themselves crosswise of the system. And in the scheme of things, she became an aberration in the firm of M. Giuliano & Associates. Never before had the great man signed on a potential superstar, let alone a woman. Over the years he had taken into the practice green young men more clever than bright, more diligent than scholarly, or competent journeyman litigators whose desire for security exceeded their ambition. Some stayed; some left after a while for various reasons; a few had distinguished themselves. His colleagues in the profession, admirers and detractors alike, advanced many and diverse theories about this dramatic turn, but Maxie had deflected all probes with his breezy wit.

"We need to get up to speed on child murders, ritual killing, that kind of thing. We're taking on that Wheeler County murder case. It's high profile and there's going to be a lot of sentiment for a conviction. There's a lot of speculation the killer mutilated those little boys, but not much hard proof, as I understand it, because their bodies were chewed up by wild dogs. Jock Dowd's pulling some things together for us and setting up a meeting with the kid and his family. Oh, I forgot to tell you, we're representing the youngest kid, the one with the Arab name...Khalil. He's Dowd's sister's boy by some Palestinian doctor. Got some problems there, too, but let's not get too far ahead of ourselves. Get started on the background. You'll sit second chair on this one. Be ready to hit the road in a day or two."

Maxie rattled free form as the young woman's fingers flew across the keyboard of her laptop. Susan concentrated on his words, getting them down as best she could, holding in mind for later inclusion collateral issues and what she might have missed typing.

"Now, get your bones out of here. I've got to get ready to convince Thornburg's boss that another one of his cases against me doesn't hold water."

Most of Maxie's cases ended in some kind of plea, bargained and sold in the marketplace of the criminal justice system. Sometimes it was justice only to the extent that a result was reached which moved the process along. This more or less subjective justice was dictated by the relationship and relative skills of the negotiating parties, mediated by trade-offs that may have had little to do with the merits of the specific case. But always in the perceived best interests of the client. It was, in the vernacular of the trade, a "disposition." Disposing of cases was the objective of the system and its traffickers: the prosecutors, the defense lawyers and the judges. Justice thus occasionally became synonymous with disposal.

Maxie brought connection, skill and weight to the table. He was thorough and persuasive. His large inventory of cases could, within limits, be marked up or down as necessary to make a deal or a series of deals. What he did was widely considered neither unusual nor unethical; he was simply better than most at working the system. And his clients rarely complained.

Back in her office, Susan continued to record her thoughts in the Macintosh PowerBook that had become her auxiliary brain and paralegal. Satisfied she was off to a good start, she broke off and punched the code for speed dial "1" on her phone, the number of the house she shared with her mother. A desultory "Hello" interrupted the seventh ring.

"Mother! Guess what! Maxie's letting me work with him on a big case. A murder! A child murder! A double child murder!"

After a long pause, Leah Wycov's husky voice responded. "You're so proud, so excited," she said. "You're defending a beast, a child-killer. My daughter, the criminal lawyer! You couldn't go into tax law or corporate. Even a good civil trial practice like your cousin, Milton. You have to work with *treyf*, with trash. And for so little money!"

Susan sighed and slumped back in her chair. Why did she expect it would ever be different? The litany varied only in its length and intensity; the content was always the same. Her mother was disappointed in her daughter's choice of a career and in a number of other aspects of her life, as well. And the money. Always the money, even though neither of the women had need for more than came from a trust fund the mother's father had set up for his children and grandchildren.

"Well, thanks for the encouragement. Guess I'll have to bear my success alone. I won't be home for supper. I'm going to do some research and meet Andie for a late supper at Sandro's."

"Wait, Honey, don't hang up." Leah was trying to darn the hole she had just torn. "I'm sure you'll do very well. Maxie has a reputation for getting people off. You'll learn a lot from him." It was less than faint praise.

"Okay. Look, I've got to go. See you in the morning." Susan hung up abruptly; she didn't want to hear the part about her choice of dinner companions. She complained to herself, half aloud. "No matter what I do, I'm going to end up a freaking stereotype. A not-so-nice single Jewish girl with a guilt-tripping mother!"

CHAPTER EIGHT

Alessandro "Sandro" Raffaeli, proprietor of the establishment that bore his name, greeted Susan enthusiastically as she entered the underlit foyer of the city's most elegant restaurant.

"*Buona sera, Signorina* Susanna. I am so happy to see you tonight."

He gave her a courtly bow and an unaffected kiss on the back of her right hand. She relished the theatricality of the gesture, thrilled that such gallantry still existed. Broad shouldered and trim in the dark, custom tailored suit, the transplanted Roman stood just taller than Susan when he straightened up. His thick black hair was going gray at the sides. The piercing blue eyes established immediate contact with hers. Waving off the maitre d', he deftly guided Susan with a subtle touch at her left elbow to a corner table where a petite, attractive blond woman already was seated, but who stood when she saw them approaching.

The women embraced warmly, exchanging real kisses at the corners of their mouths, with a lack of inhibition usually observed in children or intimate friends. They had known one another since childhood and had built a relationship on successes and tragedies, some mutual, some experienced individually and shared in confidence. They had visited seldom in the past five years, however, and had not kept up with the details of each other's lives. Through her marriage to one of its scions, Andrea Settleworth carried the name of one of the state's wealthiest and most prominent families. That bond was about to be dissolved, however, which furnished the purpose of this rendezvous.

Raffaeli, who had been standing deferentially by, held Susan's chair. He smiled across the table at the other young woman. "I have some special *caponata*, and *carpaccio* like butter, to start. Just a little of each so it does not spoil your dinner. I'll send Frank with the wine list." He bestowed a beaming glance on Susan as he turned away, silently signaling the staff to take exceptional care of this table.

"God, Susie, that man's gorgeous. And he acts like he would like to be your dessert. Is there something going on here?" Andie arched one penciled eyebrow and flashed a comic leer across the table.

"Sometimes I wish. He's been treating me this way ever since I was a kid and my father would bring me here. He's handsome; he's charming; he's bright; he's rich; and he's one of the most married men you'll ever know. I rest my case. And, while we're on the subject, tell me about you and Russell."

"Wham! Thank god I already had one drink! Well..." The cheeriness evaporated.

"Okay, okay. Sorry to be so pushy. But, hey, girl, that's me. Let's start over. Let's order some nice wine, catch up on each other, save the hard talk for later."

The women differed from one another in many ways. Susan dominated physically and intellectually. Her well-proportioned five foot ten inch body, incisive mind and assertive personality combined to intimidate even those with whom she wished to be close. She was in many ways that most fearsome of creatures: the attractive, brainy woman who challenged men and alienated other women. Andrea, on the other hand, had a doll's look and helpless little girl demeanor. She had cultivated all the right social graces. Men wanted to protect and possess her; women wanted her on their committees and in their bridge clubs.

The marriage had begun conventionally enough. Russell Settleworth and Andrea Mendenhall had met at the University of Kentucky; both moved in the upper circles of Greek social life, marked by physical excess and academic underperformance. He had money, position, and a family business in which he was certain to become a well-placed executive after an appropriate apprenticeship.

Andrea's parents had little materially, but invested in private schools, music and dance lessons, cotillion: all those things that might give their daughter an opportunity, as they would say, "to rise above her parents." George Mendenhall never rose above middle management at the newspaper before he died of a heart attack at his desk. Alice taught high school, as she had for thirty years. Her father's death benefits had taken Andrea through university and a degree in American literature, which, she was convinced, did not qualify her for any gainful occupation. Russell's parents, especially his mother, had objected to his choice of brides, but the indulged son prevailed, as he usually did, by threat and guile. Five years later, their idyll lay shattered.

Two appetizers, dinner of Sandro's veal specialty and a bottle of vintage Brunello di Montalcino later, Andie reached across the tablecloth to clasp her friend's hands. She held them tightly, seeking their strength and their comfort. Susan's long fingers pressed back, signaling a willingness to listen and not to judge. Andie lowered her eyes, released her grip and, more or less under control, let pour her troubles.

"Well, I guess I knew, should have, anyway, he'd get bored and even more spoiled. We...I...wanted a baby...He said I was his baby. He had these fantasies

– bought me these little girl clothes and costumes – never would have thought he had the time or patience. We had great sex and a lot of fun, but about six months ago he gambled pretty heavily and lost a lot of money. His mother always covered his losses, but they had a big scene this time. He stayed drunk for three or four days at a time and these phone calls would come. It scared the pee out of me. He shouted at me and said his problems were all my fault."

"Did he ever hit you?"

"No. Not that. But he might as well have. He got real abusive...you know, swore at me. Went out a lot without me. When we made love he was coarse and rough."

"Did he rape you?"

"You mean did he force me? No, I don't think so. But I got more scared and didn't enjoy our games like I used to. What really got me going was when he started hinting that he'd like me to sleep with other men. He brought a couple of tough looking guys home one night. Introduced them as businessmen from New York in town for meetings at the company. After a few drinks, he wanted me to get dressed in a cheerleader outfit with sheer panties that is a real turn-on for him. It was like he had promised them an X-rated show with me as the star. We had a hell of a fight that night. I locked myself in the bedroom. After he took his 'associates' back to their hotel or wherever, he kicked in the door and screamed that I had humiliated him. Didn't want to hear how I felt."

"What did you do about it?" Susan leaned across the table and focused all her attention on her friend's unfolding tale.

Before Andrea could continue, a voice from behind Susan interrupted them. "Well, hello, counselor, out for a little fun and games?" The alcohol edged words dropped from the mouth of Albert Thornburg, who had come over from the table where he had dined alone.

Susan spun to face the tasteless intrusion. Thornburg affected the same tone and posture he often used in court to show off the authority of his office. He leered down at the women as though he had caught them in a flagrant indiscretion. Susan glared up at him, silent; her steely gray eyes bored through him. She gathered energy as he shifted uneasily on his feet, trapped in his own ploy. A quick reaction would have let him play at being witty. She had gained the advantage by leaving him with nothing to respond to.

Addressing Andie, but looking at Thornburg with a sugary smile, Susan delivered a calm, measured introduction. "Andrea, I want you to meet Albert Thornburg — alias Absolute Thornbutt — Esquire. He persecutes criminals, and criminal defense lawyers, too, when he can. He got his name because he's such a colossal pain in the ass. He probably had dinner by himself tonight because nobody would be seen in public with him. That silly grin on his face is from the bourbon he drank to take away the taste of all the asses he kissed today."

Susan paused for effect, then continued. "Al, say hello to my friend Andrea."

The man blanched, then flushed a deep crimson. He had the look of a fish that had been hooked, gaffed, and gutted. Diners at nearby tables stifled grins and audible laughter. At least one group seemed to know him, but self-consciously looked away. Whatever Albert Thornburg had intended to say or do next, he abandoned in favor of a hasty retreat in the direction of the men's room, dropping in his wake a mumbled acknowledgment to Andrea.

"Whew! You chopped him off at the knees, Suze," Andrea said with a mixture of surprise, awe and respect. "He was off base in what he said, but I don't know that he deserved what you gave him. I'd say you don't like him."

"No, Andie. I don't really dislike him. In fact, I think he's not a bad guy, but he's got this power thing. And he's always hitting on me like I owe him a chance to get me into the sack. He just got me at the wrong time tonight. I was caught up in what you were telling me, and what I heard and saw in Thornburg seemed like the same old bullshit. Anyway, I guess there's not much use in hanging around here. You're staying at the Seelbach, right? I'll walk you up there. It's safe enough if there's two of us."

Susan settled the check, left a generous tip, accepted Sandro's obligatory but sincere *"Buona Notte!"* and peck on the cheek, and stepped with Andrea onto the sidewalk, heading south toward the hotel.

Albert Thornburg watched in furious humiliation from behind a draped column as the two women walked off arm in arm, laughing. He was chastened, but not subdued. He swore to himself: *I'll get even, you uppity bitch!*

CHAPTER NINE

Clyde Simmons, Commonwealth's Attorney for Wheeler County, leaned back in the swivel chair, looked out at the cloudless August sky, and wished he were on his boat instead of in his stuffy courthouse office.

"So, Johnny, tell me again why I should let your clients off the hook?"

"Hell, Clyde, you know these boys. They're a little wild, but they haven't killed anybody. Look, so Jared Polk and Jackie Mullins were over by the river raising some hell. They borrowed a little flat-bottomed boat from a dock on the other side and loaded it with some beer. That's all. They told me they saw this Khalil kid over by The Point. When they hollered at him he ran off."

Johnny Watress, legal jack of many trades, hunched forward as he pressed his clients' cause. His rumpled gray jacket hung open; the sweat soaked white shirt gapped across his ample stomach.

"What about the dope? I hear they'd been smoking weed. And they didn't 'borrow' that boat; they stole it. They admit they were there about the time those little Tacker boys died. We got beer cans with their fingerprints not fifteen feet from where Tellis found the bodies. Did I mention they were underage? The other boy will probably say he saw your clients there. I'm not ready to make the call."

Simmons flicked a speck of dust from his spit-shined cordovan loafers. He acted bored, as though he were engaging in a necessary formality. He smoothed the front of his tan poplin suit coat, tightened the yellow silk tie with navy polka dots against the button-down collar of his blue pinpoint oxford shirt.

Simmons was a skillful negotiator and interrogator, used to getting quickly to the important issues in a case. "Off the record, Johnny, I don't believe the Polk and Mullins boys had anything to do with the killings. But there's a lot of pressure on me because of the horrible circumstances. And I only have three suspects."

"Hell, Clyde, I hear Jock Dowd called in Maxie Giuliano to defend the Khalil boy and old Judge Dowd doesn't seem to care much what happens."

Joseph Khalil was the prime suspect even though he was Jasper Dowd's grandson. He acted strangely and had not cooperated with the investigators. Dr. Khalil had once given Simmons's daughter emergency treatment after a car wreck. But the other two were regular kids, jocks, whose fathers he knew socially and in business. He had enjoyed watching them play football and basketball the past three years. He carried his insurance with Madison Polk's agency and had bought a used pickup from George Mullins's Toyota dealership.

Simmons was inclined to steer away from the two 18 year-olds in the direction of making a more solid case against the "queer" kid. That deputy, Carnahan, had put together some damn good circumstantial evidence and was still digging. Being defended by Maxie Giuliano was a sure sign that the kid had something to be concerned about. Maxie didn't come cheap and he handled only the biggest, most visible cases, usually for clients who were perceived to be guilty. And he had a damn good track record. Rarely ever did he lose a trial, especially on a murder charge.

"Tell you what, Johnny. Give me a couple days. We may be able to work something out."

"That's great news!" Watress smiled for the first time since the initial exchange of greetings. He pushed away from Simmons's desk and got to his feet. Cigarette ashes shook loose from his food stained tie. "These boys both have scholarships to play ball and I'd sure like to see they get to keep them. We'll do just about anything you want if you take care of this."

The two lawyers' parting handshake was perfunctory. Watress had accomplished all he could hope to and rushed off to tell the fathers of his success on their sons' behalf.

Simmons turned pensive as he returned to his desk. "Connie, get me Barry Levine in Louisville." Simmons knew it was time to call on his friend and fellow Commonwealth's Attorney. He had more to lose than he could ever gain by trying this case himself and he had no assistants up to the task.

"Barry. Hey, it's Clyde Simmons. Yeah, I know you like the fishing down here. So do I, but seems like I never get out any more."

Levine predictably inquired into the progress of the child murder prosecution. The publicity had gone on past decency, but this was the kind of story the public ate up.

"Funny you mention that. I need your help. I'm getting ready to charge a kid that Maxie Giuliano's been hired to defend."

"Are you asking me to lend you a lawyer?" Barry Levine said with feigned horror, as though he were giving up one of his children into bondage. "You need someone good on his feet, used to going up against Giuliano, right? I don't know, Clyde." He continued in the same light tone, "Those kinds of people are rare and expensive these days."

"All right, Barry, a weekend at the lake. You pick the weekend. I'll furnish everything, except the women. You have to bring your own wife; I'll bring mine. Unless you want this stag."

"No. We'll play it straight. Helen enjoys the water as much as I do. I'll get back to you with a date."

Like haggling merchants, the two struck a deal, leaving out just one detail, the most important one.

Simmons turned serious. "Now. Who do I get? I really do need your best."

Levine didn't hesitate. "Remember Al Thornburg? I brought him with me to the last conference. He's sharp. From around Lexington. A Harvard law graduate. A little cocky, but he knows how to act in front of a jury. And good with complicated evidence and forensics. He could put your case together and share duties with you and your people. However you want it. Besides, he's worked a lot against Maxie and thinks he's about due to win a big one against him. You want him, you got him."

"I owe you, Buddy. I'll even bait your hook and charm the fish onto it when you come down. Thornburg, that's it, right? Have Thornburg call me tomorrow. I've got some other things to do today."

Simmons took one more look at the sunny sky. "Connie, I'm going to drown a few worms. Anybody wants me, I'm preparing for an important trial and can't be interrupted. But you can tell Mildred the truth if she calls; she might even be glad I took off."

CHAPTER TEN

Carnahan parked his station wagon in the dust between the small frame bungalow and the shabby house trailer at the back of the lot. Despite the lack of rain, steamy vapor hung about The Bottoms and filled every cranny. It was just past six o'clock. The workday was over for most people, a good time to find them home. He had tried calling earlier in the day; the Pattons had no phone and no one had answered the number listed to Millington.

The Commonwealth's Attorney's office was getting its homicide case together and he needed to talk with Matthew Patton and Rebecca Millington. The deputy's heart was not in this part of his job. How, he wondered, could he question them without setting the pitiful Matthew off into gibberish or chafing the wound of Rebecca's latest tragic loss? He had spoken to neither of them since his visit to the funeral chapel, but he knew the two mothers had called the Sheriff's office several times in varying states of upset, sometimes demanding, sometimes pleading, to know what was being done.

Matthew was the more important witness. No one had yet taken a formal statement from him, and maybe he remembered something helpful. Carnahan hoisted himself from the vehicle and trudged toward the trailer. His bad leg was aching; not a good sign. Arthritis in the knee joint piled misery on top of discomfort. He would have to get his prosthesis checked soon, maybe replaced. And the drought would surely end soon; his pain was a nearly infallible gauge.

Carnahan stepped onto the makeshift stoop and squinted through the screen door. Corly Patton and her daughters were seated at a laminate table, eating their supper, not more than seven or eight feet away. The sour odor of boiled cabbage and smoked meat rose with the steam from their mismatched bowls. "Excuse me, Ma'am, Mrs. Patton," he said. "It's Dale Carnahan, from the Sheriff's office. I need to talk to your husband."

Corly sat stone still. Jessie and Annie stared at him like startled chicks, their sweat slicked hair sticking like feathers to their scalps.

"He ain't here!" Corly said, muttering into the tabletop.

"Well, when do you expect him?" Carnahan was sympathetic but knew Patton was the kind of man who avoided confrontation at all costs and his wife was used to covering for him.

"Don't know. He got some work driving a truck. Be gone a day or two." Corly stirred, signaled the girls with a downward sweep of her palm to stay where they were, and shuffled to the door. She planted her frail body in the opening and challenged the deputy. "What you know about who killed my boy?" She didn't wait for an answer. Her rage erupted through the tattered mesh. "You got the doctor's kid and them two town boys, don't you? I hear they might let them go. Can't let nobody that evil go! The Devil was in the ones killed Billy Joe and Junie! I know. I heard. It was sure the Devil!"

The deputy backed down off the cinder block. There was no reasoning with this disturbed woman, and no purpose in prolonging either her agony or his unease. The rumors of Satanism, of ritual murder and mutilation were making their rounds; it was natural they should settle here and fester.

He responded in calming tones. "Thank you, Mrs. Patton. Please tell your husband I was by and need to talk with him. It's really important. He can help us make whoever did this pay."

"You leave my man alone! He's got enough on him without you keep reminding him. Leave us be! Get us a life for our Billy Joe's! Get us God's punishment against the Devil!" In the space of a few seconds she had transformed from beat down hound into a howling she wolf.

Carnahan retreated to the rattle of the trailer door slamming shut behind him. Shaken by the intensity of the woman's reaction, he decided not to try to speak with the other child's mother just then. As he reached for the wagon's door handle, a soft voice called to him.

"Deputy! Don't mind her. She's all torn up. Corly doesn't mean any harm."

Rebecca Millington's pale, round face, lit by the sun hanging low in the sky, was framed in the kitchen window at the back of the cottage. The deputy tipped the brim of his hat in a polite gesture of understanding.

"Mrs. Millington. I appreciate how she feels. And how you must feel. Look, I need to talk with you, too, but I won't bother you now, seeing how it might upset you. I can come back tomorrow."

"No, no. Stay on. I've been wanting to talk to somebody about it, anyways. Come around to the front porch."

As Carnahan climbed the steps, Rebecca came out the door, carrying a crockery pitcher of sweet tea and two ice-filled glasses on a wicker tray. She motioned him with a nod of her head to one of a pair of webbed aluminum chairs; they were cheaply made, but sturdy enough and clean. She set the tray on a molded plastic table between the chairs and, without asking him whether he wanted anything to drink, filled both glasses before sitting. Reacting to his look of surprise, she assured him that she kept a gallon jar of sweet tea in the refrigerator all summer long and always offered some to company.

Rebecca wore yellow cotton shorts and a loose white blouse against the oppressive heat. She seemed to Carnahan thinner and older than he remembered.

He could imagine what she had been going through. She looked over at him, demure, holding her glass above her lap in both hands. He recalled she had been the only one of the family to respond with any kind of feeling when he offered condolences at the viewing. He thanked her for her kindness, then sipped his tea and relaxed as the cold, sugary beverage trickled down his throat. He asked after her mother, Pearl Patton.

"She's sleeping. She sleeps a lot. It's the medicine. But she doesn't know much when she's awake. You know, her mind's gone." It was an almost matter-of-fact statement: one an intensive care nurse might speak.

Neither spoke again for several minutes. The stillness of creatures in the late afternoon heat echoed their silence. Rebecca shifted, tucked her bare legs beneath the chair, and spoke first. Her words were brittle, sharp as thistles. "It wasn't the dogs killed Junie and Billy Joe, was it? That young deputy at the churchyard said as much. You got some teenagers you think did it, don't you? I can't believe one of them's Dr. Khalil's boy. Dr. K looked after all of us at the clinic."

Carnahan pursed his lips. At first he avoided eye contact, then met her gaze. "We don't think it was the dogs. No. We're not sure. But I don't think we, the Sheriff's office, ever told anybody that it was. We've got suspects. Nobody's been charged but we're close. It's a strange kind of case to make. We're waiting for more information."

He said more than he had intended, but believed he was doing the right thing. Besides, there were not many secrets in Wheeler County. Gathering physical evidence and finding witnesses was primarily his job. He had done it well, but even he didn't know whether there was enough to convict anybody.

There was more work to do. The pressure on him was intense and becoming even more so.

Rebecca had nothing to add to her previous statements. Carnahan wrote out her recollections of that day, from letting her son go play with his cousin, to being told at Caslow's place what he and the Sheriff had found, then the terrible ordeal of identifying what remained of her only child. He proceeded cautiously; there was never a good way to handle these things.

Until those last few questions about the identification, Rebecca had remained composed. She was ill at ease reliving what she had tried so often in the past several days to deny, but under reasonable control. She began to sob, quietly at first, in a whimper, then let go all at once with the same intensity as her sister-in-law minutes earlier. But this was a mother's grief, not vengeful anger. Carnahan held out his arms to her. She clutched him and pressed into the hollow of his shoulder. Bitter tears overflowed onto his face where their cheeks touched.

They stayed in this awkward position until her sobbing subsided, then he guided her back into the chair and gently released his grip. She held onto his forearms, keeping him close for a few more seconds.

"I'm sorry," she said, wiping away the tears and clearing her nose.

"It's just so darned hard! I lost my daddy. I lost my man. Then I lost my baby. It's not fair! It's not right! I don't deserve it. They all three were killed by somebody else. It wasn't their fault. And it wasn't my fault. I got my momma who's addled. I've got to look after her. I've got to live with my pissant brother. I hate him for what he did. I pray. I try to understand. But I don't. I'm a good person. Why does this all happen to me?"

She paused, looked beseechingly at the deputy. "Where will I find justice?"

Carnahan had no answers. He studied her figure, filled out like a cabbage patch doll. She was not beautiful, but he found her appealing and approachable. He held out a hand to take leave; she took it in both of hers and squeezed firmly. She managed a warm smile, her first since she had served the tea. They held on to one another a little longer than might have been seemly had they been seen, but they were, in that moment, invisible to the world.

CHAPTER ELEVEN

Maxie had hired a Lincoln Town Car and driver to take him and Susan to Parkersburg so they could prepare undistracted.

"I had lunch at Sandro's yesterday. He told me you gelded Thornburg without benefit of anesthesia a couple nights ago, even though Al apparently was feeling no pain. We had a good laugh, but I'm bothered if there's a real problem between you two."

Maxie's benign manner did not fully mask his concern that extraneous issues, especially personal animosity, could impair his effectiveness as an advocate.

Up to this point, Susan and her mentor had been going over the upcoming meeting with their young client and his family. The digression surprised and unsettled her.

"He got me in the wrong mood at the wrong place at the wrong time, Maxie. He was drunk and insulting and crude and I hit him hard. In hindsight, I guess I did hit him low."

Susan lowered her eyes in a gesture of contrition but did not follow with more words. Both she and Maxie would have acknowledged the dishonesty of an apology.

"Well, there's something else I think you should know. His arrogant absoluteness is going to prosecute the Wheeler County case. Barry called me last night. Said it should be a good match up. Al's been wanting a high profile case and Clyde Simmons couldn't handle this one alone." Despite Maxie's reference to Thornburg's courthouse nickname, he spoke without humor.

Susan took his demeanor as a reproach. Had she blown her big chance because of her smart mouth and in the balance let her boss and their client down?

"Damn! Do you want me off this case?"

Maxie's face crinkled into the smile of a patient mentor. "No. You're in for the duration. And I don't want you making up to Thornburg for something you felt justified in doing. But I would appreciate it if you would not be so hard on him that he does something stupid to get even. It might already be too late. I hope not. You might think we want him to be distracted, but not so. He's predictable. He's smart as hell, but I can usually tell where he's going and can head him off. If he's trying to get back at you or me because of damaged pride or an assault on his manhood, then he's going to be erratic. He might hurt his case that way, but he can hurt us, too. I prefer my targets either sit still or move in a straight line. A pissed-off prosecutor is likely to do neither. Understand?"

Susan felt relief and gratitude for the reprieve. Mostly, she appreciated Maxie's caring to let her learn from her actions without sacrificing her self-respect.

"*Gabish!*" She expressed understanding with mock gravity in movie gangster Italian, her eyes brightening to signal that she welcomed the chance to get on with this case and her career. She punctuated her response with a firm squeeze of his hands. It was an emotional display of the kind she had denied herself since her father died.

As abruptly as he had raised the subject of Albert Thornburg Maxie reverted to meticulous preparation for the interview soon to take place, an exercise more for his protégé's benefit than his own. This left Susan no time to dwell on what had just passed between them. Or, for that matter, to think about her mother's revelations the night before. Later, in the final minutes of their journey, as the driver made his way slowly down the wide main street and around the square, Susan took in the antique repose of the small town. Long repressed thoughts filled her idling mind.

Until the summer of her fourteenth year, Susan idolized her lawyer father who, in turn, indulged her shamelessly. He had been her prince, her teacher, her friend. Something terrible was happening between her parents. They sniped at each other and, for the first time, they exhorted her and her brothers to take sides. It was then, as she would so often recall, that she realized the world was not perfect and she was not a real princess.

Leah demeaned her husband in front of the children. For his part, Susan's father turned to her in place of a wife. Over the next year she became his companion at benefits and shows, his 'date' for elegant dinners. He lavished gifts on her. The more he neglected her mother and favored her, the more Leah's resentment grew. It was from that time that Susan began to experience the small but painful retaliations of the scorned wife, the insults and slights that continued to the present. What the Chinese call the death of a thousand cuts.

Allan Wycov killed himself, but he was not a true suicide. He died alone in a hotel room. He choked on his own vomit while drunk during a siege of depression. The cause of death was listed simply as asphyxiation. Susan knew that her father had a drinking problem and was subject to wide mood swings, but she did not discover until long after his death the extent of his difficulties.

He was facing criminal charges and disbarment for taking clients' funds. Her mother had arranged through various contacts, not all of whom her daughter knew, to keep the details private, and had made full restitution. Fortunately, the investigation had been in its early stages. So far as the world was aware, a respected attorney, in the prime of his career, a benefactor of good causes, a devoted family man, had died unexpectedly of natural causes. All that was thirteen years ago of buried memory.

Seated next to her, Maxie had retreated deep inside himself and locked out all distractions. His head was bowed; eyes closed. His arms were folded loosely across his chest. Manicured fingers tapped a steady beat against his bulging coat sleeves. Even in repose he exuded the latent force of a volcano. The smoky scent of his cologne in her nostrils reinforced that image. Thoughts of the previous night with Leah now crept into her mind. *Yes, this exceptional man could switch from hot to cold and back in an instant. The Maxie you got was the Maxie he chose to be at the time, on his terms, with no apologies, no regrets.*

Maxie snapped from his reverie as the car neared the Parkersburg town limits, roused by a visceral alarm that set itself without his will. The leisurely drive through sleepy Wheeler County did not calm Maxie's concerns about the case he was about to take. More than a week had passed since the deaths of Billy Joe Patton and Junie Millington. No arrests had been made. According to Jock Dowd, pressure on the prosecutors was building like steam in a boiler. Sheriff Tellis and Commonwealth's Attorney Simmons could not much longer hold off the clamor for action. Circuit Judge Benny Willards, more politician than jurist, in whose courtroom the case would likely be tried, had called the two of them and the County Attorney into his chambers and goaded them to make an immediate arrest.

No one felt this urgency more acutely than Maxie. Word had quickly spread that he would represent the primary suspect, the one most likely to be charged, and the calls from reporters had begun. The iconic lawyer enjoyed a lofty reputation with the news media. He could be counted on for a meaty quote, for an intriguing spin on his cases. What he would say would both reflect and shape what he would do, how he would design his defense and carry it out. Out there now were only rumors, half-truths, and fanciful reconstructions of that Monday night – the rankest speculations. Themes of witchcraft, mutilation, molestation and perversion worked against him. He needed a clear sense of the Commonwealth's evidence and of his new client – pronto!

Maxie's mind was locked on immediate concerns as he entered the patrician offices of Dowd & Dowd. He had no inkling that the case of young Joseph Khalil would test his professional skills and his faith in the judicial system as no other had before.

CHAPTER TWELVE

Jock Dowd led Maxie and Susan into the conference room.

"Eddie, Jeannie Ann, this is Maxie Giuliano and…"

"…Susan Wycov, my associate…" Maxie came to Jock Dowd's rescue.

"…Joseph, these will be your lawyers. They're here to talk with us…with you…about your case."

Maxie noted with displeasure the relegation of the boy to second-class status. Didn't these people realize that he was here for Joseph, not for them, that the boy's young life stood at the edge of disaster, that their role was vicarious? Unfortunately, this was a common reaction when a minor was involved and the parents had a hand in hiring the lawyer. Maxie held back. He would set priorities in short order.

Dowd's conference table accommodated all six of them with room to spare. A secretary took requests for coffee and soft drinks as they settled into stiff, leather-upholstered chairs. The parents flanked their son opposite Maxie and Susan. The uncle took the table head to their left. Ignoring all but Joseph on whom he cast a benign but serious gaze, Maxie leaned forward, hands resting on the polished mahogany, thick fingers laced.

"Joseph...is it all right if I call you that?"

The boy swallowed, looked straight across at the lawyer, and nodded. "Sure," he said.

"Joseph, I am here to talk to you about things that may be hard for you to discuss. I am here to represent you, to defend you, if necessary, if you are charged with doing something wrong. Miss Wycov, Susan, also will represent you. Our relationship with you is very special; it is privileged and confidential. I appreciate, as must you, the love and support of your parents, but I'm going to ask them to leave the three of us and your uncle alone now." Eddie and Jeannie Ann sat erect in surprise. They looked at one another, flustered, then to the end of the table at Jock, who signaled agreement with Maxie.

"He's right, folks. This has to be between Joseph and his lawyers."

"But we're his parents. We have a right..." Jeannie Ann started to protest, holding her ground.

Dr. Khalil stood and stepped beside his wife's chair. He held out his hand to her, smiling his assent. "We'd like to wait here, in another room, Jock, no matter how long you take. We'll talk with you later." His manner was soothing, conciliatory, comprehending.

Maxie noted the mother's fire, the father's sensitivity.

As the two left the room, Susan followed and closed the door behind them. Then the two lawyers took the places just vacated by the boy's parents. Jock Dowd remained seated at the head of the table.

"Joseph, you have not yet been charged with anything. But you are intelligent and aware of what has gone on these past few days, so we will be realistic. I'm not going to ask you whether you did anything to those two little boys." Maxie might ask a client the "did you do it?" question after he had evaluated all other evidence and then sometimes only if he intended to put the client on the witness stand, a rare event. It was a judgment call that had served him well over his illustrious career and he felt confident it was the right choice now.

"But, what..." Joseph interrupted.

Maxie cut him off. "You may ask me all the questions you want. But I want you to hear me out first. Is that OK?"

"Yeah, but I don't want you to preach at me or talk down to me. I have a 162 IQ."

"Point well made. I'll respect what you ask. Please, let me go on.

"First, you must agree to let me represent you, even though your parents and your uncle have selected us. It is your choice, and I hope you will let me help you."

The boy slumped in the chair, making him appear smaller and more vulnerable. The fingers of his right hand absently clutched a square silver pendant set with an eye-shaped blue stone, hanging from a gold chain around his neck. It was the finely wrought nearly pure metal of the Levant, the home of his father's people. He nodded his understanding and assent, then spoke, almost as an afterthought. "Okay, I guess so."

Maxie smiled back, resumed. "I will not ask you if you are guilty of anything. That may come later. If you are charged, it will be up to the state to prove that you did something wrong. My first responsibility is to see that you have all the benefits of the legal system. That includes a presumption that you are innocent and keeping the prosecuting attorney to his duty of seeing that justice is done. Justice requires that you get a fair trial and that the charges against you are proven beyond a reasonable doubt for you to be found guilty. We will have access to the state's evidence before we decide what to do. I already know a lot about their case, but there's bound to be more. We have a lot of work ourselves to do. But until you are charged, I won't be able to get everything we're entitled to."

Susan sat patiently, questioning her role. She noted that "fair trial" and "reasonable doubt" needed to be explained to the boy. Maxie had assured her full participation in the case, but to this point it had been a one-man show.

Susan discreetly clicked away at the PowerBook keyboard, entering information to be organized and evaluated later. She watched their young client carefully, observed his actions, his expressions: one of the tasks assigned to her, and found herself reacting negatively without being able to pin down why. His bearing was aloof, almost resentful; his hands fidgeted in his lap when not fingering the pendant. He had pushed his chair away from the table, as though to distance himself from them. His alert eyes, squinting at times to hide their gaze, shifted between Susan and Maxie. He paid attention to everything being said, to their bodies, as though recording the meeting on videotape.

Joseph noticed how comfortable Susan was with her little laptop. He respected that. He had used computers since he was a child and had gained a great deal of skill. He fixed on the curve of her breasts and the outline of her brassiere where the top of her tailored jacket gapped, and sneaked glances at the long, stockinged legs stretched beneath the table. He may have had the brain of a genius but his hormones were right on target.

Maxie continued. "I will tell you that I am very good at what I do, and that you are entitled to the best that Susan and I are capable of in your defense. A lot of things are likely to happen. If you are charged, the Sheriff will want to arrest you. We will try not to let that happen. We'll take you to the courthouse ourselves. You are legally a juvenile, but the judge can decide that what you are accused of having done is so serious that you should be tried as an adult. The state may want to confine you – put you in jail. We'll do our best to get you out quickly, but there may be problems."

The boy stiffened in his chair at the mention of jail; his eyes widened. Maxie noted this predictable reaction and moved on without comment.

"You must not speak with anyone about anything having to do with this case unless you clear it with me or unless one of us, Susan or me, is with you. Not even your parents. Anything you say can be used to hurt you. But, that's enough for now. Let's talk about your questions."

Susan sat back in her chair, relaxed, more assured of her position, as though Maxie had read her thoughts and substituted "we" for "I" at just the right time.

"Don't you want to hear my side now?" Joseph leaned forward.

"Not yet, Joseph. We'll discuss specifics of the Commonwealth's case as we become aware of their evidence, after they bring you into the system."

The boy yielded. In fact, he was relieved not to have been pinned down. In his mind, this was a real-time role-play game in which it was up to him to confound and to defeat everyone else, a game of infinite variations, in multiple dimensions. He relished the idea of being inside the system. His legal defense was merely a subset of a greater order. He would learn the rules then twist them, subvert them, rewrite them. He would lay out alternative truths, parallel realities. He would order and reorder everything at his will. He would make himself a living virus in the operating program of the criminal justice system. He would lay traps for the lawyers. Joseph's brilliant mind raced gleefully through the possibilities. Susan's apprehension was well founded, but she did not, and perhaps might never, realize how deep and dark was its source.

CHAPTER THIRTEEN

At the same time Maxie and Susan were meeting with Joseph a similar conference was taking place across the street in the Wheeler County Courthouse. Albert Thornburg had driven down from Louisville that morning and had arrived in Parkersburg about fifteen minutes after the defense team. With him were Clyde Simmons and Spencer Parker, the Wheeler County Attorney, who would normally have jurisdiction to prosecute a juvenile. The three men had begun by getting acquainted. Introductions were cordial but brief. Thornburg was quick to mention his Harvard education. The Louisville lawyer was the new man in the case, a hired gun, but he would take the lead and dominate the case as time passed. Seated around Simmons's neatly organized desk, they proceeded to the business at hand.

"One thing's for damn sure, we're out of time. If we don't get somebody charged here in a hurry, they'll be coming after us," Simmons said.

Clyde Simmons, as Commonwealth's Attorney for the Judicial District that included Wheeler County, was especially sensitive to charges of official inaction. What had started as an apparent wild dog attack on two little boys from The Bottoms had developed into a case of murder and mutilation. It made no difference that Tackbottom was Wheeler County's wrong side of the tracks, normally of little concern to the other citizens, outrage and fear pervaded the community.

Thornburg wasted no time getting down to hard facts. "You zeroed in on this Khalil kid? I'd like to see your evidence package as soon as possible. What about the circuit judge, Clyde, what's his name? Willis? You said he's pushing you hard to get something in front of him."

Parker broke in. "Willards. His name's Benny Willards. But first this has to go to District Court as a juvenile case. Judge Carter Clay. That's why I'm here. He can waive the kid or keep it in his court. I don't think he'll keep him. And we still have to deal with those other two boys who were on the river that day. They're both eighteen. I guess it depends on what kind of evidence we have."

Clyde Simmons would have the final say on who was charged.

"So, what do you know already?" Thornburg asked this question with a hint of condescension that caused the two local prosecutors to exchange glances.

Simmons cleared his throat. "Well, Thornburg, it's all circumstantial." His use of last name address expressed displeasure, unfortunately lost on its target. "Nobody saw what happened, but we've reached a point where it looks like the most likely perpetrator was Khalil. We've placed the boy's car on the Old State Road just a few hundred feet from where the bodies were found and at about the time the Medical Examiner says they died. And he lied about being there and told a couple of different stories to investigators."

Simmons tipped back, hands clasped behind his head, and continued. "Jared Polk and Jackie Mullins were down there on the river by The Point, smoking pot and drinking beer in a stolen boat, but I doubt they did anything worse than that. According to their lawyer, they saw the other kid on the bank and kind of scared him off. But they say they didn't see the two little boys. And they didn't hang around long. I'd guess they'll make better witnesses than defendants. Besides, Johnny Watress — that's their lawyer, Thornburg — is anxious to make a deal to get them off and collect a fat fee from their fathers. They'd probably say just about anything. You know, Spence, there's nothing on the record yet about what they were doing that afternoon."

Thornburg let the reference slide. They would do what was required when the time came, including burying criminal charges in exchange for favorable testimony. He savored the opportunity to best Maxie Giuliano and that bitch Susan, and was not ready to rule out any means to that end.

"Okay. But what about physical evidence? Forensics?" Again, the irritatingly impatient tone. But the questions were the right ones.

"Look. We've pushed the laboratory people. Got great work out of the Sheriff's office and the State Police. We're still waiting on some pathology, cause of death, that kind of stuff. But here's what we have. There were traces of the four year old's feces in the Khalil car, probably picked up on the kid's shoes. If there was any mutilation, the damage those goddamned wild dogs did could have hid it. We need to put together a background on the boy; you know, past behavior, peculiarities. Should have that soon. We know he's got a genius IQ. He's big and strong but nerdy. He's capable of the kind of force that broke the Patton boy's neck. Shook to death."

Thornburg summarized. "Let's see. You've got him at the scene. Eye witness and forensic. He's physically capable. No motive yet, but working on...what? Any evidence of past violence? Cult? Satanism? That kind of thing? Who have you talked to?"

"That's where we're headed," Simmons said. "We got old Judge Dowd's housekeeper coming in to give a statement, talking to people who know him, and we've got a warrant to search Dr. Khalil's house. We'll know more later today."

"You know, that's another odd thing," Parker said. "We're talking about Jasper Dowd's grandson and the old man either doesn't care what happens or he may even be helping to nail the kid, like sending his girl over to talk to us. It doesn't make a lot of sense. He's used to throwing his weight around and he's pretty damn good at it. But not this time. And, I'll tell you. I grew up with Jeannie Ann. She was a wild one, and Dowd spoiled her good. This is real bad stuff. It's just hard for me to believe." His voice trailed off as he realized the extent to which his emotions were interfering with his professional responsibilities, a major hazard of public office in a small town. No one understood this as well as he, a direct descendant of the town's founder, the first Spencer Cale Parker.

Thornburg pressed on. "Speaking of family. What about the father, Patton? If we don't have a motive or eyewitness to the deed, he could be a suspect."

"We thought of that, Thornburg. We know the odds. But it didn't seem to fit. Anyway, before the Sheriff picked up that line, the case started to build against the Khalil kid. It seems real solid. Besides, we both know that the motive book is out the window. Crime makes less sense every day. Especially killings. Look at all the random shootings. A lot of the hitters are kids younger than 16. It was a fourteen-year-old gang-banger got Deputy Stubby Carnahan's leg with a "street sweeper" and that was before all this heavy-duty crap that's been coming down in the past three or four years. Hell, everybody's a potential murderer and everybody's a potential victim." Self-serving as it was, Simmons's explanation was both plausible and accurate.

"What kind of a defense will we get from Giuliano?"

"One that I can predict for sure. Maxie will point out every possible alternative to our choice of defendants and the father will be right up there

85

near the top, along with those two jocks. Let's get Patton's statement ASAP!" Thornburg knew the opposition well.

Parker chimed in. "That will hurt us, won't it? You know, that we had other suspects."

Thornburg reproached his colleague. "Don't you think it would be a lot better to explain that we investigated then eliminated them, rather than have our asses hanging out like a bunch of baboons?"

A tight-lipped Spencer Parker took the rebuke like a chastened schoolboy.

Thornburg riffed through his notes. He made a final entry "tie up loose ends," then closed the leather binder. "How much of this stuff is out yet."

"Nothing official, but there's a lot of talk," Simmons said. "It's hard to keep secrets around here. We think Jock Dowd's been keeping tabs through his sources and passing information along to Giuliano. After we break up here we'll go down to Paul Tellis's office and get with Carnahan. He's a real good man to have on our side. He can show us his file and answer a lot of your questions."

Clyde Simmons stood and stretched. He pressed his hands into the small of his back to ease the stiffness of long sitting. He looked out a window that opened on the south side of the square just as a group of people stepped onto the sidewalk from the Dowd Building.

"In fact, there goes our cast of adversaries now. That stocky fellow must be Giuliano."

Like a six-year-old at the sound of a siren Thornburg rushed to the window. Half hidden in shadow, he peered between the slats of faded wood blinds. He focused intently on the enemy. He tensed when he picked Susan Wycov's shiny, dark hair out of the small crowd. He nearly overlooked Joseph, but fixed on him as he walked a few feet west and entered a Buick sedan with a man and woman Thornburg assumed to be the boy's parents.

Already he was building the image of a brutal murderer he expected one day to sell to a jury.

The young prosecutor's agitation was not lost on the two local attorneys, who had already concluded that something way beyond a desire to see justice done motivated their new colleague.

CHAPTER FOURTEEN

Susan had stayed late at the office, preparing to accompany Maxie the next morning to meet with their new client in Parkersburg.

"You're late! Supper's cold! The one time you tell me you're going to eat at home, I cook and you don't come!" Leah Wycov had reacted predictably, filling the air with hurt.

"Mother, I called. Don't be so touchy. Warm it up and we can sit down together if you want. I suppose you haven't eaten, either."

Susan knew it was futile to apologize. The only way to respond to her mother's neurotic behavior was to be direct, to move things forward. Leah's ability to dredge up past transgressions was more than sufficient for both of them or, for that matter, for all the generations of Wycovs and Cohens.

God! What a drudge you are! Susan grimaced at the weary face in the mirror. She traced with the polished nail of a slender index finger the lines beginning to show around her eyes and mouth – the "sags and bags" inherited from her father's side. She enjoyed what she did as a lawyer, but the rest of her life took a beating. Scrubbed and changed into shorts and a tee shirt, she took herself back downstairs. She found the dining room table formally set for two in the Royal Doulton china and Stieff sterling, with the added extravagance of lighted candles in a heavy silverplate candelabrum.

Whether the overdone ceremony was Leah's atonement for an earlier tirade or another labor to be added to the ledger of a life spent in servitude to her family was not clear. In either event, it was no longer of concern to Susan, who had taken to accepting her mother's actions at their face, as she did the needlework Leah stitched and displayed unabashedly for all to see. The ever-present quotes and pious maxims augmented the mother's pitiable carping. They created for her a private reality of word-images she alone chose and interpreted. Leah had, for all practical purposes, sewn herself into a cocoon of self-righteousness, within which she could do no wrong.

Leah refused help serving the meal, so Susan took her place at the right of the table's head, which after her father's passing her mother had appropriated for the few occasions when the dining room was used, mostly on holidays. Supper began in silence, overhung by the toxic cloud that formed whenever mother and daughter were together and which choked communication between them. Susan took an embroidered linen napkin from a silver ring and winced as she read the neatly hand-stitched message unfurling across her bare thighs: *"How sharper than a serpent's tooth it is to have a thankless child."* Leah, by way of King Lear, had got in the first dig.

Susan was not about to comment on the napkin's reference and she did not want to talk about work. Any mention of Maxie Giuliano or her choice of careers usually triggered a barrage of sarcasm and thinly disguised contempt. And, even if she had a social life to discuss, the conversation would inevitably turn to marriage and babies, subjects not especially high on Susan's priority list. She loved her mother; that she knew with certainty. But she could not easily locate that love within herself or express it in any satisfactory form. She smiled self-consciously, revealing, despite all her strengths, the intimidation she felt in Leah's presence, and determined that they should get through the evening with as little new damage as possible.

Leah looked at her daughter and began, sweetly. "I talked with Jerry today. He said Sylvia has been trying to call you to invite you this weekend. He thinks you're avoiding them. Your own brother. I stood up for you, though. I told him how busy you are and I never see you either." She smiled, smugly, in control, then turned casually to cutting a warmed over piece of roast chicken on her plate.

Mercifully, the daughter had just taken a mouthful of soggy salad greens and was excused from making an immediate reply. The oily sweet and sour dressing adhered to the roof of her mouth. She chewed slowly, deliberately, then took a long sip of over-chilled Chardonnay. Her mother and brothers conspired against her regularly. The invitation was probably intended either to introduce her to some "nice young man" (young anymore meant under 50) or to encourage her to reconsider her choice of practice specialty. Even in these enlightened times an unmarried sister or daughter could be the object of well intentioned but unwelcome meddling. Pondering her response, Susan let her eyes wander around the room. They settled on a large sampler, vividly embroidered in crimson, one her mother had sewn years earlier and mounted on the wall across from where her older, and at that time notoriously wild, brother Jerry usually sat at table. *"Sin in Haste, Repent at Leisure."* It was a classic Leah Wycov rendering, reflecting her particular reality.

Susan decided to follow that advice, savoring the irony. She charged ahead.

"Mother, you're right, my work keeps me very busy. So I won't inconvenience you any more. I'm moving out. Next week. Besides my regular caseload, Maxie has put me in charge of preparing for that murder case in Wheeler County. I'll spend a lot of time over there; probably stay in Lexington. He has a lot of confidence in me."

Susan delivered these words matter-of-factly, slowly, in modulated tones, as if asking her mother to pass the salt. Moving back had not been her active choice. She had remained at the urging of her grandmother, Bubbe Annie, and her brothers. Although thoughts of leaving had long been harbored, this announcement was spontaneous. She had no idea where she would move to. She had planned to get a furnished efficiency or a room in a motel when the time came, but there was no way she could now recant, nor would she. Leah would whine and plead, cajole and threaten, as she usually did, but in the end would don the martyr's robes of the scorned mother and grudgingly accept the accomplished fact. To compensate she would elevate filial ingratitude to the top of her extensive list of complaints — again — and stitch a new sampler.

Susan's announcement caught Leah just having put a slice of chicken into her mouth. She raised her head and froze for an instant. Her heavily made-up eyes narrowed and she slammed the heavy silver fork down on the tabletop.

"Maxie Giuliano!" The name exploded from her lips in a spray of spit and half-chewed meat as she sprang to her feet.

"You trust that greasy son of a bitch? You're sleeping with him, aren't you? You'll leave me, your mother for that ungrateful Dago!"

Susan shrank in her chair, stunned by the unexpected vehemence of the assault, an extreme of her mother's personality she rarely saw. Her composure withered under the onslaught.

"Are you crazy? This has nothing to do with Maxie. Just me and my work." Susan's voice quavered.

Leah leapt from her chair and hovered like a harpy above her daughter, poised to tear flesh from bone. "You don't know anything, you little slut. I should have told you, but no, I wanted to be a good mother. You break my heart every day, but you just put a knife into it and twisted it. That man screwed up my life. Two times, the lousy bastard. And now three…"

As Leah railed, Susan's courage began to return. Her curiosity was aroused, but she wasn't sure she wanted to hear more. "I don't have to listen to this crap!"

Susan tried to stand. On her feet she would physically dominate her mother, giving her an advantage in what had become a decidedly one-sided conflict.

Leah pressed down on her daughter's shoulders, just hard enough to keep her from rising without a struggle, then abruptly released her grip.

"Oh, my God! What's happening to me?" Her voice trailed out in a keening wail, a legion of demons fleeing a tormented soul. She clutched her hands to her face and fell sobbing against the wall.

Susan guided the hysterical Leah back to her seat. Stooping over her, she daubed mascara-smeared tears with a dinner napkin. Neither woman spoke. The outburst had lasted barely a minute and Leah had now closed up inside herself. Susan realized that she had just witnessed the manifest agony of an embittered woman and, with the return of equilibrium, was determined to hear the whole story, or at least so much as her mother could be induced to tell. Whatever the facts, her own relationship with Maxie could be greatly affected, but how and to what degree she would not speculate.

The dining room cleared, mother and daughter relaxed in the overstuffed intimacy of Leah's combination sewing-reading room, christened years before by her children as Mother's "I want to be alone" room. Leah had subsequently memorialized it on an embroidered banner crediting the Swedish actress Greta Garbo with her famous line from the film "Grand Hotel." Two partially consumed glasses of wine rested on the table between them. The dam of silence having broken, Leah let pour the acrid waters of her tribulation, and, in the course, would fill for Susan some of Maxie's hollow spaces. Leah's mood was mellow, relieved.

"Maxie and I go way, way back.

"Maxie and your Uncle Sammy played together when they were kids. They were about the same age, five years older than me. They went to law school together, too. I remember always wanting to tag along with them. They would chase me away and Maxie teased me. He called me 'Bambina.' That's Italian for baby. I would get so mad at him. 'I hate you, goy boy,' I would holler, then run away. I had a mouth on me even then. What was I? Five or six? Then our family moved from downtown to the Highlands and we lost touch for a long time.

"In college I was an activist. Rare at the time. U of L was a real streetcar college and nobody but the Greeks much cared about what happened when classes were over. Anyway, I got elected to the University Student Senate in my junior year and pushed for all kinds of causes. One of the big issues was affiliation with the NSA – National Student Association - a real liberal group. Maxie was president of the Senate; he was in his last year of law school. In those days he was a real Neanderthal when it came to politics. He had a big chunk of iconoclast in him, but he supported a lot of the status quo, too. Oh, he satirized the tight-ass administration and the Old-South orientation of the school and the community. He did a wicked dean of men. But those were the fifties, Eisenhower time, and the waves were all small and local."

Leah leaned back, eyes closed, mellowing as she retrieved long stored memories.

"So, when the issue of NSA came up, he put me on a committee, but just to keep things under control, he made himself chairman. We fought like hell. We didn't agree on many things. But he never was rude or mean. Ideology never seemed to play into his arguments, though, not like me. I felt strongly about almost everything. I really fell for him. He was such a commanding personality. Smart, articulate, persuasive - and I thought he was really good looking. So he wasn't very tall and he was shaped more like the base of the statue than the man with the sword, he still charmed me out of my socks.

"Maxie led the delegation at the traditional Christmas party the University president held for members of student government. He didn't seem to date a lot. He spent whatever time away from class and being a Big Man on Campus working and helping out his mother. Anyway, the party was dry, and some of us wanted to go for a drink afterwards. Maxie had this neat Chevy coupe and I needed a ride. We just kind of ended up together. He told me I made myself such a pain in the ass it was easier just to take me with him."

Leah paused to refill her wine glass and held the bottle out to Susan, who waved it off. She had neither her mother's love of drink nor her tolerance for its effects.

"About one in the morning and a lot of beers later we parked in front of my house. We just sat there and talked for a long time. He told me he wanted to be the best criminal defense attorney in the country. That he wanted to make sure the system did its job. It was funny. He didn't seem all that driven to help people, although he had a reputation for being generous. He wanted to test his skills against the system and in that way he might dominate it. It was kind of like he didn't want to be the bull, he wanted to be the one who led the bull around by the ring in its nose. I thought it was queer at the time, even through the alcohol. He was such a talented leader, but he didn't want to run anything - just make sure it ran the way he wanted it to. Is that too obtuse, Honey? I'm not sure I can say it any better than that."

"Mother, I get the picture. It's the way he really is, isn't it? He has achieved so much and has ingratiated so many people to him. But you know, you're on the mark. It's like the rest of the world is a circus and he's the ringmaster. He doesn't want to own the circus or do the high wire act. He wants to direct traffic and take the bows. But he acts so modest and humble…Now you've got me doing it. I'm not sure I'm making any sense, either."

Susan shrugged in mock confusion and reached for her glass.

"So, we sat and talked, facing each other across the front seat, our backs against the doors. He turned off the motor. When I started to shiver, he offered to turn on the heat or, he suggested, maybe I wanted to go in. Instead, I asked him to hold me. To stay a little longer. I didn't know what to expect but, honestly, I had...well, I had the hots for him and I had to start somewhere."

With that admission Leah giggled as though she were sharing an indiscretion with a girlfriend the morning after. It did not dawn on her that her actions of nearly forty years ago seemed naive today. But Susan sat in wonder at this new dimension her mother was revealing. A vulnerable girl was hiding inside the cynical woman.

"He didn't say a word. He just opened up his coat and motioned me to slide across the seat. I leaned my body into his and laid my head against his chest. He folded the coat around us and began to smell my hair. 'You remember when I teased you so much?' he said. 'You know, when Sammy and I didn't want to be bothered? I liked you then, like a ten-year-old would, not understanding why, showing you attention in a bratty, smart-alecky way. I guess what I really liked, deep down, was the way you took up for yourself. When your parents moved away, I think I missed you as much as your brother.'

"He was talking into the top of my head. Like he had something to say but not just to me. To himself, too. More to himself than to me.

"I slid my arms around him and turned my face up to his...God, Susan, this sounds like one of those Harlequin books - I can't believe I'm saying all of this." Leah's eyelids drooped; she was losing steam. "I haven't thought about these things in years and now..."

Not about to let her mother stop, Susan said, "Mom, you crap out on me now and I really will move out. If you don't finish the whole damn story I'll put it to Maxie and get his version."

The threat had an invigorating effect on Leah. She drew her legs beneath her on the cushion of the overstuffed chair, lit her umpteenth cigarette of the night, and went on.

"He kissed me and I kissed him back. I don't know what he was expecting, but I Frenched him. He stiffened up and pushed me away, like he was a virgin and I was after his goodies. Well, I was still a virgin but, like I said, I wanted that man. For the first time he seemed unable to find words, and what he did next devastated me. Here was this twenty-four-year-old man who turned to stone. He closed up his coat and sat bolt upright, both hands on the steering wheel, staring out the windshield. He didn't even say 'Goodnight'. He just waited for me to let myself out of the car and go into the house.

"What could I say? I wasn't sorry about what I did, so I was damned if I would say it. I thought he was a real asshole, and I did say that. And a few other things I meant then but regretted later. The tears poured out of my eyes, I guess as much out of hurt as anger. He sure as hell didn't seem to care. He didn't budge. I got out and slammed the door. I could swear he flinched then. But I was crying and tight and as soon as I was clear, he started the engine and pulled away from the curb. Slowly. I guess that's what pissed me off more than anything else. He acted like I no longer existed. No emotion. That's what really broke my heart.

"After that, whenever we saw each other, always on campus, always around other people, he acted polite, friendly, joking. For him, nothing seemed to have happened. For me, there was pain. I told myself I didn't give a damn. But I did."

"Excuse my two cents, Mother, but sad as that is, if that's all there was to it, how does it merit all these years of anger? And I always thought he and Daddy were good friends."

"Yeah, and there's a hell of a lot more you don't know." Leah's tone hardened; her mood turned sour. She uncoiled herself and walked into the kitchen. On the lamp stand beside her chair a boat shaped ceramic ashtray overflowed with crumpled butts. Ashes dusted the tabletop. An empty goblet stood in a drying claret ring.

Susan heard a cupboard open and close, something scraping across a countertop, water running from the tap. She did not get up, did not turn around. She stared outside into the road, where a streetlamp glowed violet through the windowpanes. Did she want to hear more? Was this just petty unrequited love or tragedy playing out over the years? Susan feared most that she would end up judging her mother, taking sides against her. Not just for Maxie, but for herself, her dead father, for all the other oppressors against whom Leah claimed perpetual victimhood.

The evening had come full circle, starting and ending with the two women on different pages, perhaps not even in the same book, as their views of life diverged so dramatically. Susan rose, wobbly from an excess of wine, and shuffled to her room, not stopping to say good night. It was nearly midnight. She had to meet Maxie at seven in the morning for the drive to Parkersburg and the start of a journey whose life changing consequences she could not have begun to imagine.

CHAPTER FIFTEEN

Sleep did not come easily. Eddie and Jeannie Ann Khalil lay back to back at the opposite margins of their large bed, not touching, not speaking. Each had staked out a haven, a place to regroup and to plan, leaving between them an uncrossable plain. Their minds replayed the day and previewed imaginable futures. Their disparate visions brought them neither comfort nor assurance.

After the morning meeting with the lawyers, Eddie had dropped his wife and son at the house, on his way to see patients in an adjoining county. "We'll talk more about this when I get back," he had said. The drive from town had been especially strained: Jeannie Ann full of questions; her husband urging patience; their son closemouthed and distant. The mother sought answers; the father craved order; the son wanted only to be left alone.

Down the hall, Joseph's room sat vacant, stripped of the boy's trappings and possessions. Three sheriff's deputies, accompanied by two of the state's lawyers, had taken posters off the walls, books and magazines from shelves, clothing from pegs and drawers, shoes from the closet, and the computer and storage disks from a desk. A Nintendo player and cartridges had gone into a cardboard box and down the stairs. A framed photograph of the boy with his paternal grandmother was lifted from the dresser and added to the harvest. They had taken Joseph away in a car with blue lights flashing, in a parade of flashing blue lights. They had come, they announced to his mother at the door, to execute a search warrant, to seek and to take evidence relating to the killing of the two little boys by the river. The father was unreachable on his car phone and remained unaware.

The deputies and lawyers had completed their search and confiscation and were huddled around their gleanings in the breezeway, speaking in whispers. The tall attorney in the gray pinstripe suit seemed to be in charge; his back was to the kitchen door from which they had exited. His voice rose above the others', his right arm swung in a wide arc, encompassing the physical evidence and ending with his outstretched hand pointing into the house. They broke; some sort of decision had been reached. Two deputies and Clyde Simmons began carrying bags and boxes to vehicles parked in the driveway. Albert Thornburg, followed by Deputy Dale Carnahan, reentered the kitchen. The prosecutor had shifted from suspicion to certainty, from polite formality to righteous reprisal.

Jeannie Ann, wound tight with fear and indignation, stood a few feet away by a counter, eyes locked on the two men. She planted herself between them and her son, sensing Thornburg's change in mood. The boy, perched impudently on a stool behind the counter, stared at them as well. He grinned smugly, as though he, not the lawyer, was in charge.

"Mrs. Khalil," Thornburg began, flashing a folded paper, "We're taking the boy with us. I'm charging him with murder. He..."

Jeannie Ann sprang at the lawyer and erupted in his face, "The hell you will! You get your ass out of my house - now! I'm getting our lawyer back down here before I let you lay a hand on him."

The ferocity of the assault and the spray of spittle in his face forced Thornburg backward, off balance. In an almost comic collision he banged into Stubby Carnahan, who reached out instinctively, embracing the larger man to break his certain fall. Instead of accepting the deputy's help and regaining his balance, Thornburg thrashed with his arms, turned in a way that took both men crashing to the floor, and knocked a wooden chair clattering against the wall.

Hearing the commotion but not knowing its source, the other deputies charged through the door, their weapons drawn and leveled above their colleagues' tumbled forms, aimed at mother and son. Joseph, who had jumped to his feet at the initial confrontation, threw up his arms and yelled melodramatically, almost gleefully, "Don't shoot! I confess!"

Jeannie Ann gaped at him in horror, speechless; her body went limp.

"You what? What did he say?" Thornburg said from one knee. Not so upset he could not react, the lawyer barked at Carnahan, "Give him his rights! Give him his rights!"

Stubby's artificial limb had twisted in the fall and hampered his return to his feet. One of his fellow deputies pulled him up. It was with a disquieting mixture of satisfaction and distaste that he cuffed the boy and took him into custody. No one had worked as hard as he on this case, but he took no pleasure in the arrest.

In the back seat of the patrol car, seated next to a relaxed and unintimidated Joseph, Carnahan thought through the significance of what had just gone down. The young man's outburst disturbed him. On its surface, it was damaging as hell, and Thornburg had leaped to take advantage of this stroke of apparent good fortune. On the other hand, it didn't fit; the kid was practically laughing out loud at his and Thornburg's pratfall. He seemed to react not so much out of fear of being shot — the drawn guns made the scene more surreal — as to take control of his own arrest. The few words the boy spoke at the start of the ride were perfunctory — matter-of-fact comments and questions that might be expected of an inquisitive tourist on a sightseeing bus. Carnahan's responses had been professionally neutral — concise and to the point, neither hostile nor cordial.

A stab of pain shattered the deputy's concentration; he rubbed his leg where the prosthesis attached. He thought about what might happen next.

I'm glad I'm not defending this kid. As far as I'm concerned, everything we have points to him. If he did it, he's one sick puppy, and I hope they put him away for a long, long time.

Paul Tellis was waiting at the back steps when the caravan arrived at the Courthouse, County Attorney Spencer Parker by his side. County Judge Joe Beeler looked down from a corner window on the third floor. He had not been invited to the party and wasn't sure at this stage that he wanted to attend. Patty Anderson saw the emergency lights from her desk at the newspaper and ran across the street, reporter's pad in one hand, a Nikon camera in the other. She got off a whole roll of exposures before the phalanx of officials and their prisoner disappeared inside, ignoring her repeated pleas for a statement and closing the door in her face. She scurried back to her desk in the *Democrat* Building and punched long distance.

CHAPTER SIXTEEN

"Maxie, how long you been back from Parkersburg?"

The lawyer hesitated, unpleasantly surprised by the speaker's knowledge of his whereabouts and irritated by the insinuating tone of the question.

"Griggsbie, what the hell are you talking about. Are you in the bag already?" Maxie played dumb. He knew that the reporter on the other end of the line would not make this call unless he had something. Harry Griggsbie was too good at his craft and had enjoyed the benefits of too many exclusive stories to play coy.

"You know your client's been locked up? They took him in not thirty minutes ago."

An even more upsetting surprise. "You got a stringer down there, somebody at the *Democrat*? What did you hear?"

"You really didn't know that, did you? I'll be damned! This must be a first. Look, I'll share if you will. This story will play hot and long and I want to bat first and stay in the game until the last out. Deal?" Had he not turned into a Pulitzer Prize winning crime reporter, Harry Griggsbie would have flourished as a sportswriter. His head took him down one path and his heart drew him to another.

"You show me yours first." Maxie's jaw tightened. He reached for a pen.

"Half the sheriff's office and a crew of lawyers, including your pal Al Thornburg, brought Joseph Khalil to the courthouse in a show of flashing lights. He was in handcuffs, by himself. If he's made a phone call, it obviously wasn't to you. My source tells me the grandfather and an uncle are heavy hitter lawyers down there. You working with them?"

Maxie demurred. "The kid's a minor. You can't use his name yet. It's a circumstantial case, but something crazy must have happened in the past couple of hours. I've just got back and things seemed quiet enough." He paused, scowling. "I must be getting old, Griggsbie. Stuff like this doesn't happen to me!" It was a glimpse of mortality: the reluctant admission of an exceptional athlete who got left a half step behind or swung a split second too late.

"Knock off the self pity, stud. It's a bad fit. You understand I have to print something. My source isn't exactly exclusive. But I'll just say you were unavailable for comment. Now, am I on your team? Usual rules?"

"Sure. You get to lead off and bat cleanup, too. I got to find out what's going on. I'll talk to you tomorrow. You call me. Oh, yeah, thanks…I think." Maxie's mind had moved on to his next call.

"Yes, Maxie, Joseph's been arrested! I was just getting ready to call you. How did you find out?" Jock Dowd's voice projected a mixture of irritation and embarrassment.

"The media knew about this before I did!" Maxie's displeasure spilled through the phone. He had tracked Dowd down at home.

"Sorry about that but I was busy finding out what happened." Dowd apologized not for the delay in contacting his nephew's lead attorney but for taking, not making, the first call. "They're holding him as a juvenile, so you know we can't get him out right now. But, old buddy, I found out that Simmons knew you were here this morning. He was parleying with Albert Thornburg and Spence Parker at the same time. Sounds like they wanted to sidestep you. They had a warrant, searched the house and took a lot of stuff from the kid's room. Clothes, books, pictures, his computer. Jeannie Ann's spitting fire.

"The bastards! That really pisses me off. I guessed they might play hardball, but not this early. We'll get right on it."

"And, Maxie..." Dowd paused and cleared his throat, "...I'm not exactly sure what happened, but, according to Jeannie Ann, when they arrested Joseph he confessed!"

Maxie choked back his exasperation. It was not unusual for clients to ignore his warnings about talking to the police, but he thought he had the boy's attention. Maybe he should have taken more seriously Susan's unease. He prided himself on his ability to read people, especially criminal clients, all of whom he assumed to be liars, but something in the boy's manner had eluded him. Joseph had been so attentive and respectful. Maybe too much so. A pang of inadequacy stung him again.

"Old Buddy, you still there?" Jock Dowd had expected an immediate response.

Maxie recovered quickly. "Yeah. Jock, I don't want to overreact. We just need to get our arms around what's going on. Let's file for a detention hearing. Get me the dockets for both Carter Clay and Benny Willards, for all three counties in the Circuit. And the grand jury schedule. Can you take care of that right away?"

"I'll get one of my girls to fax them up to you first thing in the morning. And I'll hold hands until you and your associate - Susan? - get up to speed."

Maxie dwelled for a moment on the ramifications of the just ended call then hollered out his open door.

"Willie Mae, get me Susan!"

CHAPTER SEVENTEEN

Joseph spent the first night in the county jail, a dreary and decrepit warren of concrete block yellow-tiled rooms and iron barred cells in the basement of the courthouse, segregated from adult offenders as the law required. His guards had permitted visits with his mother and father and his uncle, Jock Dowd, who acted for the time being as the boy's lawyer until Maxie could get into action. Despite Jeannie Ann's raging threats and Eddie's forceful urging for immediate release or relocation, nothing was done. Assured, however unconvincingly, by Jock and Sheriff Paul Tellis that tomorrow would bring relief, the parents reluctantly returned home.

The detention center resembled not so much a jail as a rundown dormitory, poorly ventilated and under lit. Joseph had eaten the fast food supper brought in by a deputy, amused by the "Happy Meal" box in which it arrived. He sat on the edge of the steel-pan cot, the only furniture in the small, dim room, reconstructing and, as was his way, reordering the past few hours. He had endured his arrest and confinement stoically, despite the attendant clamor. He had ridden in the patrol car aloof as a celebrity being chauffeured in a limousine to an awards ceremony. All this uproar existed just for him; he was its center.

Beyond the initial commotion in his mother's kitchen, he had been treated gently and almost deferentially. Only in Albert Thornburg, who had identified himself when the search warrant was served, did he detect any pleasure at what was happening. In fact, Thornburg acted as though he had just scored a game-winning touchdown and could not resist spiking the ball. Joseph knew of no reason for such an in-your-face reaction, but he would find out why the prosecutor seemed to take his arrest so personally.

I'm inside the system. I wanted it. Now I have to win. Joseph reached to his throat for his grandmother's charm. His hand closed on emptiness. He felt a sudden, naked chill, the shivering fear of a lamb shorn and staked out for slaughter. He had indeed started something he must finish. He had lied about using the car because that was his nature. He had lied again to the deputies because he felt superior to them and to his parents.

His "confession" had been both calculated and spontaneous. When confronted with the search and eventual arrest, Joseph knew that he must not surrender control of the process - the game. His best tactic was surprise, an ambiguous act that would confound his foes and at the same time bring him into full participation. It had freaked his mother out and would piss off his hot dog lawyers, but he wanted to direct their roles, as well. As for that pompous prosecutor, he would fall on his ass more than once before Joseph "Saladin" was finished.

It would not do for him to be only a passive object. The script was his to write or revise. He would construct his own spaces and furnish them as he willed, even if bound within someone else's domain. He would, by one means or another, prevail. He would get close to Susan, who would admire him for his cleverness and intelligence, and fall in love with him! His fantasy turned erotic.

"Your lawyer is here to see you." *The voice was not one he had heard before. Susan stood in the doorway, smiling, naked, looking at him with hot eyes, her tongue rolling across her lips, inviting him to have sex with her, if he thought he was man enough…*

The illusion faded as quickly as it had formed and fatigue overcame him. Joseph was certain he wanted to go forward with this game, but as he fell asleep conflicting thoughts warred in his mind. The shell of his self-confidence cracked just enough to admit into his dreams the twin demons of doubt and dread. He was, despite his intelligence and cleverness, still only sixteen years old.

CHAPTER EIGHTEEN

Mattie Bernly fidgeted in the hard wooden chair. The depleted seat pad gave her little comfort. Tobacco leaf hands clutched the worn black leather bag that filled the hollow of her full-skirted lap. She sat erect, almost stately. She would speak forthrightly, with the passion of conviction that she could speak only the truth.

An overly solicitous Clyde Simmons leaned toward her from the edge of his seat at her right, one arm resting on top of the conference table, across which sat Albert Thornburg, scratching notes with an expensive ballpoint pen on a yellow legal pad. A tape recorder rested a few inches away from the questioner and his witness, tended from the head of the table by court reporter Ima Crofton, who would redundantly record what was said in a fine, furious shorthand.

"Now, Mattie, I know you want to help us find out what happened. I don't want you to say anything you don't know for sure, but it will be better if you just answer my questions when I ask them. We'd be just as happy as you to find out that the boy had nothing to do with this business."

No one in the room, with the possible exception of the witness, believed the prosecutor's last statement. Under other circumstances, in another case, perhaps, a patina of objectivity might overlay the deposition, but Thornburg had left no doubt that all stops would be pulled to get a conviction. This faithful old Dowd family servant would, wittingly or otherwise, set the mood within which a jury would consider the evidence.

The preliminaries done and the old housekeeper set at ease, Simmons glided skillfully into the heart of her testimony.

"Now, Mattie, you know that day they found those two little boys, Billy Joe Patton and Junie Millington dead over by The Point?"

"I remembers that awful day."

"You know that Joseph Khalil has been charged with killing them?"

The old woman looked away and in a sad, hesitant voice, said, "I sure do know that, and it ain't right, ain't right at all."

The first set of questions dealt with what Mattie had experienced on the day of the crime. "Yes, I was ironing sheets for Miss Jeannie Ann at the little house and I seen Joseph go out the back door and get into the car - the red convertible. I looks at the clock. It's exactly three minutes past seven o'clock. I always likes to know what time it is. No, he's not supposed to drive it without first his Daddy or his Momma say it's OK. He gone for about an hour. I hear the car when he pulls up and looks at the clock - eight nineteen – then out the window. Well, Joseph gets out the car and wipes off his feet in the grass next to the driveway and comes back in the way he left then he go the back stairs to his room. Yes, he acts kinda funny, like he knows he done something he shouldn't. But I suspicion he just didn't want them to know he took the car when he wasn't supposed to. I didn't see him no more that evening. I went back up to the big house to look after Mr. Jasper."

"Okay, Mattie, you've worked for Judge Dowd and his family for thirty years. In that time, have you had occasion to observe - to be around - any of Jeannie Ann's husband's, Dr. Khalil's, family?"

"I told you I looked after the boy since he's a baby."

"No, I mean anyone else, like the doctor's parents or other kin."

"Sure enough. Doctor Eddie's momma from overseas come to visit three or four times. I think his daddy been dead a long time. One time she bring a pretty young woman with her, the doctor's sister. She called Rema. But that's a ways back."

"Tell me about his mother. You get to know her when she was here?"

"Oh, yes, I knows the Old Lady. I calls her that. She acts like she's a queen. Dress real funny, but serious, like she's wearing glory robes, only all black. Wears a scarf around her neck. And her head she all the time holds up high and she looks right through you, like she know what you're thinking. Doctor, he calls her 'Umma'; Mr. Jasper just say 'Old Woman'. She's different. You know, like a hoodoo woman. An' that boy - he worships her. An' she looks after him good, too."

"What do you mean 'hoodoo'? Like a witch or something?"

"Something like that. My husband's people from Louisiana. I seen them in the bayou make things happen you don't want to see. You don't want done to you."

"So, tell us some things she'd do or say." Simmons looked over to see the other lawyer's eyes popping, his writing hand poised - eager, like a hound on the scent.

Mattie Bernly paused, her back straight against the rigid slats, eyeballs rolled back reflectively, searching her mind for images, for words. "Well...Oh, I remember, too, she got those tattoos on her hands, like circles and little dots, blue. Like signs. I never asked her what they for. Anyway, she act like she's a wise old bird. Don't speak English too good, but when she want

111

something, she let you know. She talk to Doctor Eddie and the boy in that lingo...

"In Arabic?" Albert Thornburg interrupted, oblivious that he had spoken out of turn, but not out of character. He responded to his colleague's glare with a careless wave of the hand, his consent to continue.

"I' m sorry, Mattie, you were telling us about the boy's grandmother and..."

"Well, she, the Old Lady, she speak that A-rabic to the doctor when she don't want nobody else to know what she saying. She teach it to Joseph, too, so's he can understand her and he can talk it to her. But she knows what people say. I can tell."

"What else would she do? You said she acted like a witch. You mean like evil?" Simmons's tone betrayed a native impatience aggravated beyond its usual limits by Thornburg's animated reactions to the questioning. There was not much room for digression.

"No, not evil. But she did believe in the evil eye. She told me one time, best she could, with the boy helping her, that there was people give the evil eye, 'specially to children. It was when they envy something and want it. She give Joseph a big old silver and blue stone charm to hang round his neck. He never took it off far's I know. She said a blue stone keeps the evil eye away but she could fix the eye if she needed to, and she could give it, too, if she wanted to."

"Did the boy believe in this...evil eye, as well?"

"He sure act like it. Whatever the Old Lady told him, it was like gospel. He give his momma and daddy and his granddaddy fits, but he minded the Old Lady and, rest her soul, Miz Libby, too, his other grandmother."

"Was there something else she did that made you believe she had, uh, strange powers, or at least acted like she did?"

"They was one time. Last time she come over here, maybe five, six years ago. She boiled this awful black coffee, like mud, in a funny brass pot. Jeannie Ann ask the Judge and Miz Libby to come down after supper and I come with them because Miz Libby was feeling poorly and I was setting up with her some. So, the Old Lady serves this sweet pastry, and this coffee. And after she pour out the coffee in these little bitty cups and everybody drinks it...Well, it's more like poor Judge Dowd and Miz Libby was being polite and they sipped what they could and Miz Jeannie teased her Daddy so he drink some more till they's just a lot of grounds in the bottom of the cup. I was watching all along so's nothing bad would happen to my family.

"The Old Lady hand me a cup, but I just put it down beside me on the table and didn't touch a drop. So when they finishes the Old Lady pick up everybody's cup - except mine - and turns them over in the saucers. Judge ask what she's about and the Doctor say she's gonna tell everybody's fortune from the grounds. Well, Mr. Jasper he laugh and Miz Libby smile real big and say, 'I can't wait to hear what's going to happen to me.' Well, you know she was talking about getting over her misery, but the Old Lady pick up her cup first and turn it right side up and just stare into it for the longest time and talk her talk to Doctor Eddie real fast and soft and he tell Miz Libby the Old Lady say her flower garden gonna bloom big this summer and her friends be jealous.' Now, this was good news, because Miz Libby got the greenest thumb and she belong to this garden club with the ladies from her church and they was always trying to outdo each other. Then she tell Joseph he gonna do good in school, but he always done good in school, so that was no news. I just sat there feeling like she sure didn't know nothing special.

"Last she get the Judge's cup and she get this look on her face, like she see something awful. She set it down like it was on fire and jabber something quick as lightning and Doctor he say to the Judge that she can't tell anything because it's too cloudy and she was just having fun with all of them, anyhow.

But I don't believe that and sure the Judge don't either, but he don't say nothing about it. Just stand up, say it's late and Miz Libby needs her rest and packs us up the hill to the big house without so much as a good night."

"Is that all, Mattie? Isn't there more?" Clyde Simmons's disappointment was obvious. He had gone after bass and pulled in a sunfish.

"There sure enough is. I found out about it later. One day after the Old Lady gone back over the water, I was down at Miz Jeannie Ann's tidying up and Joseph come home by himself after school. The curiosity was killing me about the Judge's fortune and I asked the boy what he knew. Well, he look at me straight and he say he heard what the Old Lady said to his daddy and he understood most of it and he didn't want to believe what she said. I told him he needed to tell me because I was responsible for this family. So he come up real close to my face and he say real low, 'She said my Granddaddy Dowd did something real bad and that Grandmother Libby wasn't gonna get well because of it.' I let out a holler and dropped the pan I was holding and fussed at that child for his meanness telling me such lies. And he started to crying and say 'Mattie, I'm not lying, but please don't tell anybody what I said. It's awful and I don't know what to believe, but my Sitti doesn't lie.' I got scared myself because Miz Libby getting worse and the Judge acting real out of sorts himself. I suppose 'cause he's so upset about Miz Libby being so sick." She took a breath.

Encouraged, Simmons pursued the question. "And what happened next?"

"Well, Miz Libby never got better and the doctors in Lexington couldn't tell her what was wrong and she got the most beautiful garden anybody ever seen and then wasted away and when the first frost took the last flowers, the Good Lord took her sitting in her upstairs window looking out..."

Mattie Bernly pulled up, breathless from the intensity with which she had delivered these words. Tears furrowed her copper colored cheeks but she made no move to wipe them. She just stared ahead as though she had witnessed the fulfillment of an evil prophecy and only in the telling was the vision made whole. In her mind the vision became an irrefutable truth.

"Just one more question, Mattie, then you can go home. What do you really believe happened?"

"I know the Old Lady put a spell on Miz Libby. I don't know why. And she lied about Mr. Jasper. Nobody ever hear no talk he done something so bad. Ever. I hear some hoo-hah about a white trash stable girl. But I don' believe it. I would of known he'd a done it. He's a hard man, but he's a good man. And no man ever loved a woman more than he did Miz Libby. I think the Old Lady knowed about how the Judge never took to the Doctor or cared much for his grandchild and she wanted to punish him. And the boy believed her awful story. Poor baby, poor baby! Under her spell! And my poor Miz Libby, just wasted away." Mattie's voice trailed off.

For several long moments the room was silent except for Thornburg's shuffling the pages of his pad, riffing them like so many playing cards. The session seemed to be at an end. Then, as though from a trance, the old lady began again to speak.

"Then there was those cats..."

The old housekeeper's story would take on the sanctity of a declaration of faith. Properly managed, her account would nail down one of the corners of the prosecution's box, a coffin made to measure for young Joseph Khalil. The lawyers were well satisfied; the day had ended as they had hoped it would. And they had no doubt that, when the time came, Judge Benny Willards and his jury would pay close attention to Mattie Bernly.

CHAPTER NINETEEN

"How did I get the name, Maxie? Well, that's classified information. Only on a need-to-know basis." Maxie's square face crinkled with mischief. One thing he did better than keep a confidence was tell a story, especially on himself.

"What is your need to know, young lady?"

Susan took up the challenge. "How about I'm dying of curiosity and if I check out now you'll lose the best and most brilliant associate you ever had. Then, before I go I'll leave Absolute a note implicating you in my death and he'll indict you. By now he probably wants your ass as badly as he wants mine. So, how's that for 'need'?"

"You make a pretty convincing argument, counselor, but I can't say much for your ethics." He responded as much with pride in his protégé's ability to spar with him as with the pleasure of sharing what he brazenly called "Chapter One of the Maxie Giuliano Foundation Myth."

"Okay," he began, "When I was a kid I took a lot of ribbing about my name. You know, 'Mary-O', 'Mary', 'Maria', all kinds of variations, like it was a girl's name. I was very sensitive, but my father insisted 'That's your given name, after my Pappa - you no be ashamed of it.' What did he know? He didn't go to school with me. Right?" He embellished the monologue with waves of his hands and his precise mimic's skills.

"When I was about 12 years old I had this gym class and we were learning the muscle groups. This one day, I showed up for class in a new pair of gym shorts. My mother had got the idea because we all had to wear blue ones with white tee shirts that I should have my initials on everything so I would know which ones were mine. 'Mario,' she said, one hand tugging at my ear lobe, These pants cost fifty cents and you're not gonna lose 'em. *Capisce?*' So she sewed a white tag with 'MG' across the seat of the shorts - on the outside! At least she marked the shirt on the bottom of the tail.

"This was a real hoot for the rest of the guys — none of us needed much excuse to make fun, anyway — and they gave me a hard time about it. I was chunky and broad across the beam. That just made things worse. Did the letters mean 'Mario's Giant-sized shorts' or 'My God, what a big ass'? They tried all kinds of M and G combinations. Then one wise guy got it. 'Hey, I know what it stands for,' and he pointed to the anatomy chart on the gymnasium wall, to the words *gluteus maximus* printed across the illustration's backside. 'Maximum Glutes.'

"You can guess the rest. 'Maximum Glutes' became 'Maxi Glutes' and then just 'Maxie'. At first I got angry. Then I tried to ignore it. Finally I realized that the name had a tough sound to it and seemed to fit me. As I got older nobody remembered how I got it, anyway."

He turned serious.

"When I got to high school, I put my name down as 'M. Giuliano', then let everybody think my real name was Maxie. It hurt Pappa's feelings when he found out, but I didn't hear about that until a long time afterwards."

"What happened?"

Maxie hesitated then went on.

"My Pappa wasn't the talkative kind. He didn't say much and I grew up not asking him questions. Over the years I pieced together from what he would let slip, a story or two from Uncle Pete, then right after he died, Mamma filled in a lot of the gaps. I knew I didn't have grandparents, uncles or aunts. I thought it was just part of the immigrant thing. You know, a new life in '*Lamerica*'.

"Well, she sat me down after the funeral. The first time I saw her cry. She told me my father was a good, hard-working man, and I should remember him and respect him. 'His ways were his ways,' she said.

"I asked her what she meant by that. 'You ever hear of the Big Earthquake in Calabria? In 1908. A hundred thousand people died. Maybe more. Nato was fourteen years old. He left his village near Reggio, went to Naples to find work as a stone worker, sent money home. He was there when the ground opened up and swallowed his family. They never found the bodies, his father, brothers, sisters, mother, uncles, cousins, neighbors, all gone. Not even a stone over them. They were farmers and laborers, poorest of the poor; nobody cared about what happened to them. He stopped believing in God, almost died from his grief.

"'When I got pregnant with you, he told me this. 'If a boy, his name is Mario after my Pappa'. He tells me. 'He will be the only family I got.' Yeah, he was my husband, but you were his family. The hope of his people. I was his breeder. But you never forget to respect him. He never said anything to you, I know. He never said nothing to nobody. But he loved you, had pride. You gotta know this. When he found out you called yourself Maxie, he tells me, 'that boy spit on his grandfather's head.' But he never said nothing to you. Till the day he died, he never said nothing to you.'"

"I never knew whether she told me these things to enlighten me or to shame me...or to vent her own unhappiness. That was the first and the last time she ever spoke to me like that. From that day until she passed on, she never again talked to me about my father. She went every week to the cemetery. I know she prayed for him. But she didn't utter his name to me. Even when she asked me to drive her to visit his grave, it was 'Maxie, come on, we gotta go to San Tomaso'. To the St. Thomas Catholic cemetery."

He stopped speaking, looked past Susan at the wall, at nothing in particular, into infinity. His eyes misted. She sensed he had not told this story many times before and wondered at his digression, this impromptu *mea culpa*, or so she perceived it. And why to her?

Maxie recovered, brightened, continued. "Anyway, Kiddo, that's how I got to be Maxie. Now, here's a dollar."

He reached into his top drawer, pulled out a crisp single and laid it in Susan's palm.

Susan crumpled the bill next to her ear. She flattened it, held it close to her face and turned it over, examining it as if it might be counterfeit. She even sniffed it.

"What's this, hush money?" she chuckled.

"Close. I just retained you and put you under the attorney-client privilege. You tell anybody this story and I'll have you disbarred." He said it with a straight face.

Then both client and attorney broke into hearty laughter.

"By the way," Maxie shouted at Susan's back as she was going out his door, "The guy who picked the name grew up to be a best-selling author. Says I was his first work of fiction."

119

CHAPTER TWENTY

Joseph was used to being alone. Even when around others he withdrew into his own mind — into the company and comfort of his intellect. The boy had greater affinity for computers and made-up personae than he did for real people. So the remote world of online gaming suited both his intellectual and his social needs. Denied a computer, he began to form in his mind a reality both alternative and superior to his present circumstances.

Susan had asked if he had ever in the past intentionally injured another person, or even an animal, anything that could be considered malicious. Joseph knew the kind of prior act that she meant. Had he ever tried to hurt other kids or killed or tortured pets or other animals? And if he had, he added to the exercise, was it something the prosecutors could find out - and use against him? One episode came vividly to mind. He recalled it in near perfect detail.

Joseph had waited until the adults had all gone downstairs, then slipped from his bed. He curled up in the rocking chair placed in front of the original double-hung, nine-paned windows that overlooked his grandmother's garden.

The late-afternoon light bathed and warmed him. Joseph focused on a distant line of trees, half in vivid autumn foliage and half stripped to bare limbs, the wavy old glass bending the view with kaleidoscopic effect each time he moved his head. A stomach virus had invaded his nine-year-old body the night before, so his father had medicated him and ordered him to bed for the day. The vomiting and diarrhea had ended, leaving him hungry and eager to return to his favorite pastime: rooting about the house and land in a compulsive quest to learn all he could about all there was. He believed that everything and everybody concealed something meant for him to seek out and discover.

He and his parents were staying temporarily with his grandparents while their new home was being built on an out parcel of the farm. Actually, it was more a gentleman's estate than a farm: thoroughbred horses, Black Angus cattle, a sizable tobacco allotment, feed crops and pasture. Grandfather Dowd made a substantial living as head of the venerable family law firm and held numerous profitable interests in business and real estate.

The main house, a large red brick Georgian style mansion, was a vault of secrets, things his parents and grandparents kept from him, hidden away in locked rooms, in drawers and boxes, in cellar and attic, and in the minds of those who lived and worked there. He assumed it was because they thought he would not understand. In truth, because of his intelligence, they feared he might understand too much, too well and too soon. The grounds and the garden, his Grandmother Libby's pride and treasure, were, however, places where secrets begged to be uncovered. From an early age, he was able to discern the gross and subtle differences between the world of nature and that of human construction.

A gray squirrel scrambling from the canopy of a nearby pin oak grabbed the boy's attention, although at that moment it would have taken much less than that to distract him. Near the base of the trunk it paused in its

121

downward dash, lifted its head, looked about, and sniffed the air in that twitchy, cautious manner of rodents. A single acorn filled its mouth. Satisfied that no enemy lay in wait, it raced across the ground and crouched in the shelter of a large, low urn flanking the narrow path that led to the water pump at the south end of the garden. The squirrel rose on its hind legs, tail erect as a cornstalk, and again scouted nervously about. Then, in a single elegant leap, it cleared the lip of the urn and landed among twigs, the remains of leaves and assorted debris, damp from an afternoon shower, one of those chill October harbingers of winter.

A headless dandelion spread forlornly in the center of the urn, a remnant of summer, the consequence of either his grandmother's oversight or nature's whimsy. With one more vigilant look around, the furry creature set about its work, to cache its prize against the lean pickings of the months to come. Furiously the sharp foreclaws tore at the black soil, spewing dirt and litter behind, disappearing into the excavation like the bit of an augur. Joseph barely suppressed a laugh as he watched the scrawny digger in action, its brushy tail whirling.

As the squirrel labored below, Joseph reached for the pellet gun he had received the previous Christmas. He seated a steel ball in the chamber, then pumped the lever until the backpressure stopped him. Slowly, cautiously, so not to alert the adults or alarm his quarry, he raised the lower sash until it would accommodate the barrel, which he slid across the white-painted poplar sill. Handymen had removed the mesh screens and stored them away until spring.

Its treasure hidden, the creature filled the hole as diligently and aggressively as it had dug. Like tiny trowels, its forefeet shoved, packed and smoothed the spoil in graceful coordination, eliminating most traces of disturbance. It was a closure worthy of Ali Baba's cave.

The boy aimed, aligning the rear notch with the tip of the front sight. The pellet launched with the snap of clapping hands. An instant later, the squirrel straightened and turned abruptly toward the rim of the urn, poised to leap. Instead, it toppled limp as an unstrung puppet over the edge and onto the gravel. It lay there, still.

Joseph took small satisfaction in the killing, for that was merely a means, necessary, but just the means, not the objective of his action. He was conscious only that he had taken sole possession of the squirrel's secret, and it pleased him. He had no idea what he would do with this knowledge; he knew only that the destiny of the acorn in the urn had passed to him. He could let it be found by another foraging creature, sprout to a seedling that would be uprooted and discarded, or he could dig it out at his whim and actively determine its fate, for possession of the knowledge was possession of the thing itself.

"Joseph Khalil, are you out of your bed?"

His mother's voice from the bottom of the back stairs startled him into action. He heard her footsteps on the rubber-padded treads and listened for the creak of the second stair from the top that would signal her imminent arrival at his doorway. In practiced haste he closed the window, repositioned the chair and dove beneath the quilt, dragging the air rifle with him.

"Gosh, Mom," he said, "I just woke up. Is something wrong?"

Jeannie Ann leaned over the bed and pressed the back of her hand against her son's forehead. Joseph's face was flushed and damp but she seemed satisfied that he had no fever. Some instinctual mechanism, a mother's equivalent of radar, flashed a look of suspicion. Joseph tensed. His mother sighed, apparently relieved that he was rapidly recovering, and said nothing. She kissed him on the cheek and smoothed the covers, barely missing the gun barrel that nestled alongside the boy's left leg.

After his mother had gone downstairs, Joseph clutched the turquoise charm that hung on his chest and said a silent prayer of deliverance. Killing a living creature for no good reason was not a small transgression in the Khalil and Dowd families. Joseph could only hope that some scavenger would carry off the evidence before his grandmother visited her garden in the morning.

Joseph rushed to the window at first light. The carcass was gone. He found himself both relieved and disappointed. The tension between concealment and disclosure, between deception and detection, excited him.

It thrilled him still.

"No," he said, turning back to Susan. "I don't think I've ever done anything like that."

She took from a thick folder the statement of Vincent Martin.

"What about the lab cats?"

The boy's eyes popped with surprise and a hint of respect.

"Who told you about that? That dorky Vince. Right?"

"He wasn't the only one. I can't decide whether you were just being a good businessman or you really enjoyed catching and 'preparing' those poor creatures."

"It was fun. And I got five bucks apiece. When your Dad's a doctor, you pick up some things that come in handy. I can't help it if that stupid school couldn't supply the class. And nobody ever asked about where they came from. I think they didn't want to know."

"How many did you get?"

"About ten or twelve. That's all. Not a big deal."

Susan noted his lack of concern. He displayed no remorse at having hunted strays and asphyxiating them. She could draw no hard conclusions. It could be innocent or evil, a matter of perspective. No, not innocent. That was the wrong take. Not white. Not black. A definite shade of gray somewhere near the middle.

"Now tell me about the combat games."

Susan was referring to Joseph's history as a fantasy role-playing gamer, particularly in the alter ego of Saladin, the great 12th century Muslim warrior. It was an activity in which he excelled and, so far as she had been able to discover, found great pleasure. She might have to defend Joseph's conduct. It would be helpful to Thornburg as he put together his theory of guilt. And he would probably find it out on his own.

CHAPTER TWENTY-ONE

The woman's manner was cool and professional. "Remson Academy, office of the Headmaster. How may I help you?"

"Please tell Mr. Fortinbras Albert Thornburg is calling." He mimicked the secretary's obliging tone.

"The Headmaster is not available right now. May I know the purpose of your call?"

"No, you may not. He is expecting my call on a confidential matter. Tell him I am on the phone." Thornburg spoke in crisp, authoritarian syllables.

The line went silent, but not dead. The call was being transferred.

"Thornburg, quit hardassing my assistant." The voice was jovial, familiar.

"Hell, Larry, you and your kid brother taught me that a Princeton sheepskin carried special privileges. Maybe I learned too well."

"No, Al, it took a JD from Harvard Law to make you into a real asshole."

"OK. I yield. This could escalate to full-scale class warfare and I'm in a hurry." Thornburg shifted from forced cordiality to hard business. "What can you give me on Joseph Khalil? Conduct, friends, class work, problems. You know. Was he a weirdo or just one more maladjusted bright rich kid entrusted to your tender ministrations?"

"You're playing catch-up, old pal. Some lady lawyer was up here last week, right after fall term started, and gleaned the fields. She paid me a visit. She was a good-looker and an even better interviewer." The Headmaster's words rang with gleeful mischief at this chance to tweak his overbearing friend. "She spent a lot of time with Vincent Martin, as close as Joseph has to a best friend, and with some of the boys in the advanced computer program. These are some of the nerdiest but brainiest kids we have here. Joseph specialized in fantasy role-play games."

"What the hell is that, some kind of perversion?" Ignorance of an apparently significant matter exacerbated Thornburg's ill temper, aroused by the thought of Susan 's having beat him to the punch.

"It could be. We let the students have virtually free rein with the computers and some of them spend half their lives on the Internet playing fantasy games with people from all over the world. They call their groups 'MUDs', MUSHes, MOOS. You name it; they have an acronym for it. Some of their games get pretty violent. Kind of cyber 'Dungeons and Dragons.' You do know what that is, don't you? Medieval fantasy combat. Only a lot more complex and freewheeling. It's good that they are just connected electronically. I understand Khalil is very adept and a major participant. His specialty is Saladin and the Crusades. There's a lot more to it, I'm sure. You may want to come or send someone up if it's all that important."

"Of course it's important. I've got two dead and mutilated kids and Khalil fits my profile. If I can document conduct..." His voice trailed off. "Look. I'd better make it up there right away. Can you give me some extra help?"

"If you mean access to his official records. Not even for you without some kind of court order. I can arrange for you to get access to the other students and our faculty, though. You should be able to get a pretty accurate picture from that. That is, if you are as good as Susan Wycov. She left here in a pretty happy mood."

Thornburg winced at the other end of the line. "Sure. She probably banged you and half the upperclassmen." His humor was strained and off the mark.

Larry Fortinbras did not offer a direct rejoinder, but got in one last barb before hanging up. "Let my assistant know when you're coming. You made such a good impression, I know she'll be eager to please you."

The headmaster's sarcasm sailed past the self-absorbed lawyer. Despite, or maybe because of, his intelligence, Ivy League education and physical good looks, Albert Thornburg had managed to let ambition obscure his basic humanity and humility. Since election as governor of Boys State his senior year of high school, he had made no secret of his desire to occupy the real office as Kentucky's chief elected official. His skills in debate and organization had served him well and continued to carry him along his chosen path. He had clerked for a judge of the 6th United States Circuit Court of Appeals and practiced briefly in a prestigious Louisville-based regional law firm, having declined the offers of Washington and New York firms in favor of the political fast track. He chose to build a reputation as a prosecutor and form political alliances as his path to the statehouse.

The chief assistant Commonwealth's Attorney's slot was made to order. He had served only a year in the trenches of lesser felonies, advancing rapidly because his demonstrated abilities and political connections impressed his boss, Commonwealth's Attorney Barry Levine. Levine was nearing the end of his six-year term and let it be known that he wanted back into the cushy and well-paying world of civil practice. He had been part of a coalition of upstarts who took it upon themselves to reform local government and was the group's sole survivor of bitterly contested primary elections.

Normally, Thornburg would rely on Commonwealth's detectives or a junior attorney for investigative and research legwork. In this case, though, he had a contact and would make sure he got what he wanted.

Remson Academy specialized in the education of young men like Joseph Khalil: highly intelligent, socially inept, independent-minded and from well-to-do families. Relatively new among exclusive prep schools of high reputation, Remson encouraged independent study and supplied its students with excellent current technology to be used in its well-balanced curriculum. Writing and speech courses supported the near universal obsession of its charges with what was commonly known as the Cyberverse.

It was in this setting that Joseph honed his skills, exhibiting an exceptional talent for literary creation and the articulation of abstract ideas…and where Albert Thornburg would fail to grasp how this might affect his prosecution of the case and its attending consequences.

CHAPTER TWENTY-TWO

Rebecca Millington stood in the front doorway of her cottage, watching the road for Stubby Carnahan's station wagon. A light breeze blew the first few fallen leaves across the yard. Pearl Patton sat comfortably nearby, dressed by her daughter in Sunday finery, sedated, docile. Her sister-in-law and nieces would join them on the drive to worship at the Bethel Fellowship Church.

In the weeks following the horrifying death of her child, Rebecca had grown close to the deputy sheriff. Their relationship, begun formally in an atmosphere of grief and sympathy, had progressed to what might pass for a traditional courtship, cautiously pursued, driven more by need than passion. It was not that they felt no physical attraction. The woman's emotional wounds had not healed and her fundamentalist Christian beliefs, reinforced in the aftermath of tragedy, discouraged intimacy. Ethical concerns nagged at Carnahan and constrained him. The mother was a potential witness and, in his mind, as much a victim as the murdered son. He tried to walk the thin line between professional duty and personal feelings, not always with success.

Two Saturdays before, he had discreetly taken Rebecca to a movie and dinner in Lexington, after which they lingered on the porch where they had first experienced mutual attraction. They spoke of loss and healing and, in the intimacy of the moment, he told her details of the pending prosecution of Joseph Khalil. She accepted that the case was circumstantial, built one block at a time, but pointedly inquired about Joseph's motive, there being nothing that connected him with the dead boys before that terrible day.

Carnahan shared with her the discovery of Joseph's fantasy role-play games, the Saladin persona, the evil eye charm and the stray cats caught, killed and sold to college students. Rebecca recoiled at the implications of such conduct, at its inherent depravity. She had put off Corly's raving insistence that the Devil's hand slaughtered their children. Now, she perceived a connection, an evil force directed at her flesh and blood.

Rebecca's revulsion and consequent hysterics ended the evening. No consolation — by word or touch — could calm her. He left cursing himself for his careless candor, for his foolish breach of confidentiality.

Carnahan pulled onto the unpaved drive. Five females awaited him on the narrow porch: Rebecca and Pearl had been joined by a sallow Corly Patton and her snuffling daughters, whom he had not expected. Their presence weighed heavily on him, as though he were being cast in the role of the families' avenging angel. Matthew Patton was predictably absent. Carnahan had not seen him since that day in the funeral parlor, and did not ask after him now.

The drive was tense, quiet and mercifully brief. Rebecca fidgeted next to him in the front seat and avoided physical contact. Her eyes scanned the road ahead, even when she spoke the few words to pass between them. Carnahan wondered cynically if she feared he carried a communicable disease. The old lady lacked her customary incoherent prattle. He guessed it was from a heavy

131

dose of medication to keep her still during services. Corly and her girls might as well have been tree stumps planted in the back of the wagon.

A turn off the county road and a mile long drive up the pocked blacktop lane brought them to a flat place carved into the roadside, where sat the clapboard meeting house. Carnahan had not been there before. He noticed from a distance how poorly maintained the building seemed, needing a fresh coat of whitewash and repair of cracked and rotting boards. Asphalt shingles sagged with the roof joists. Weeds grew in profusion where the bare ground did not show through.

On the signboard in the front yard, beneath the names of the church and its pastor, in faded removable letters, he read: "Today's Sermon: SATAN WALKS AMONG US PRAY FOR OUR CHILDREN". The theme caught his eye. Was this why he was invited to come to meeting on this particular Sunday?

The other side of the road drew Rebecca's attention – the ill-kept churchyard where her son, her husband and her father lay buried.

A front pew had been reserved for the family. They filed in, Corly first, her girls, Rebecca, Pearl, and on the end, Stubby Carnahan. Their collective mood remained grim and edgy despite the compassionate pleasantries of those they passed on the way in.

The Reverend Dewey Cadwell – Brother Cadwell to his flock – greeted them soberly. He gripped Carnahan's hand firmly but fleetingly, in the ceremonial manner of a politician working a crowd. Carnahan studied him, looking for the qualities that drew Rebecca Millington and these others to his ministry. He stood about six feet five inches tall and looked down at the deputy through nearly colorless irises as piercing as lasers. Sandy brown hair straggled over his ears, branched down acne scarred cheeks in coarse sideburns and fell across the collar of the ill-fitting black polyester suit. His voice was pitched high, accented from somewhere south of Kentucky, maybe

Alabama, but with sharper inflections. To the deputy he seemed young for his calling, rough cut yet confident, charismatic. A latter-day Abraham Lincoln wannabe.

Brother Cadwell was calculating in the entrepreneurial way of small time preachers whose congregations gather like stands of wild mushrooms in dank woods, their fragility and brevity of life to be speedily exploited. Above his flock he erected a canopy of scripture and bombast that promised salvation in its shelter. As recompense he demanded adherence and a portion of their material little.

Services opened with a greeting, a blessing and two hymns. The second hymn sung, the people sat. The white-robed choir, seven women and five men, took seats on folding chairs set in two rows against a side wall, facing the lectern. The accompanist was Sister Minnie Cadwell, the wife of Dewey, a plump, ruddy, youngish woman dressed in a plain black frock, long-sleeved and high-necked, trimmed in cheap white lace at the throat and cuffs. She shifted on the padded bench to face her husband, a sign of readiness to receive his words.

Brother Cadwell officiated almost casually from a shallow platform upon which stood a lectern draped in purple cloth. His gangly body dominated the narrow nave, aligned with the pine-planked aisle parting the two rows of pews as if by divine command. He stood silently, scanning the sparse assembly, not more than sixty souls in all, his mesmerizing gaze fixing each of them briefly as it passed over.

"Satan walks among us! Satan walks among us! Satan walks among us!"

The preacher began softly, slowly, thrusting his head forward over the lectern. With each repetition, the pace of his words quickened; his voice grew louder and rose in pitch. The final "Satan" roared from his lips.

Rebecca stiffened, her fingers tightening viselike on the pocketbook in her lap. Corly drew her weeping girls to her. Pitiable in their suffering and isolation, the three huddled together as a single being. Carnahan sat straight-backed at the end of the stained oak pew, keeping an almost clinical composure. As he would for the duration of the sermon, he listened to the words and fought off the emotions they invoked. Indistinct murmurs rose from the assembly.

"Two of God's innocents, lambs of this flock, were brutally slain in August. We buried their frail, mangled bodies. We mourned them. We grieved for our loss. We prayed for their souls. For understanding. For forgiveness. We denounced their slayer. We pleaded for justice. Would that it was enough! We know now it was not just random, cruel and wanton murder, horrible as that may be.

"It was an abomination, wrought by the very hand of Satan, the Evil One, through his demon spirit in this world. His name – the name of this son of Satan is – Joseph Khalil!"

A shiver crept into the preacher's voice as he intoned these words. Sobs rose in the hall, loudest from the front pew where the grieving mothers relived the horror of their loss. Carnahan reached his arm around the old lady to touch Rebecca's shoulder. She shrugged him off and rocked mechanically in her seat, holding a handkerchief tightly to her mouth, sealing off an anguished cry. Corly Patton held her daughters even more closely.

Brother Cadwell caught his breath, gathering energy. With his voice and his gaze he fixed in turn each man, woman and child, challenging them.

"Idolatry…Sorcery…Blasphemy…Desecration…Mutilation…Murder!" The litany of transgressions tripped from his tongue with the intensity of a swelling drum roll.

"The Joseph Khalils who play computer fantasy games, who practice witchcraft and idolatry, who mutilate and murder for pleasure believe they possess power. They are mistaken. They are imprisoned in dungeons of bondage from which only Jesus can free them. We must make a great noise against those who indulge in these games, who permit them to be played, who defend those who do evil, who are silent in the face of these violent and unholy practices."

A chorus of "Amens" answered him.

"When these people commit violent acts, is it because they are acting out a fantasy life? Do they believe society's rules do not apply to them, that they are free to create worlds of their own, where they make and remake the rules to suit their whims? Does familiarity make them insensitive to pain and death? Do they practice violence as a way to deal with life?

"Joseph Khalil spends his life in 'virtual reality', which he distinguishes from 'real life', his reference to the society of real – not made up – people. People like you and me! Joseph Khalil calls himself a god. He casts spells. His favorite is the 'Evil Eye,' a curse of great power, steeped in superstition and paganism. Joseph Khalil has taken unto himself the diabolical persona of Saladin, an Arab and a Mohammedan, who slaughtered Christian men, women and children and desecrated Jesus' Holy Cross.

"Joseph Khalil killed for fun! Yes, for fun, as a game. He murdered and maimed in the fantasy worlds he created. He committed violence for its own sake without fear of punishment. How many times has Joseph Khalil killed for pleasure?

"Why would he kill and dismember for the fun of it?" Dewey Cadwell let the question sink in.

"Because he could bring the dead back to life! The maimed he could make whole with the tap of a computer key!

"Until one day Joseph Khalil came upon two defenseless little boys playing on the banks of the river in the real world. The world in which true believers live. Did he slaughter Junie Millington and Billy Joe Patton for fun? For his own evil pleasure? For the pleasure of his master, Satan? For the pleasure of watching them die?"

Each question was posed rhetorically, spaced for full effect, bearing the answer within itself.

"Whatever Joseph Khalil's motives, we know one thing for sure: neither he nor any power on this earth or in his fantasy world can make their broken bodies whole or restore their lives to them!"

The evil other had been named and the case for his condemnation made. The preacher breathed deeply in sympathy with the horrified gasps of his flock, in thrall to him and his words. He wiped his brow with a large white kerchief he pulled with a magician's flourish from a suit coat pocket.

Building to a climax, Brother Cadwell drew himself to his full height, the embodiment of a Biblical judge, and lifted his eyes and arms to heaven in supplication. His words reverberated like thunder within the four walls of the narrow nave.

"O Lord, we call upon You to cast out this spawn of Satan! We beseech You to strike down false gods! You are the one God. Your son Christ Jesus is the sole mediator between God and man. There is but one resurrection for the salvation of souls!"

Drenched in sweat, his voice worn to a raspy undertone and his breath laboring, Brother Cadwell filled the hall with an intermitting silence. He lowered his arms and gripped the sides of the lectern, dropping his eyes for a moment to the Bible lying open there. He looked up and spoke softly as a loving parent to his children.

"Why do you sit there weeping, nodding your heads? Accept Jesus Christ as your personal savior. The only reality is in Him. It is not virtual reality. It is not fantasy. It is not a game. He sees through us. There is no disguise He cannot pierce. No thought He does not know before it is formed. The only immortality is in Him, in His salvation. Be born again in Him!"

"Take refuge in your faith, for thus are you saved by the gracious gifts of God. Speak out, all of you, God's people, against the evil practices of this apostle of false gods. This Joseph Khalil! It will not restore to us the innocent lives so brutally taken – we take comfort that they are with their Lord in heaven – but it may save other innocent lives."

Head bowed, eyes pressed shut, he concluded in measured tones.

"Let us pray.

"Heavenly Father, shield us from the Evil One. Protect our children. Save them from the sins of the mind that lead to sins of the flesh. Heal us as a people. Keep Your teachings ever before us that we not be led astray, for You are the one true God. Let Your power be shown before all men. Strike down the idolaters and the blasphemers, the maimers and the murderers of this world. In Your Son, our Lord and Savior Jesus Christ, is the only resurrection and life. In His name we ask these things. Amen."

It was what Rebecca Millington wanted to hear and in vindication what she took away. For his part, Stubby Carnahan wished himself on another, far away planet.

CHAPTER TWENTY-THREE

Maxie phoned his sometime adversary and always friend, Jefferson County Commonwealth's Attorney Barry Levine, to make him an offer he would be too intrigued to refuse.

"Barry, we can do each other a favor. Got some time tomorrow morning?"

"I may be a winner! Is this Publishers Clearing House? Haven't we put you out of business yet?"

"You read too many Mr. District Attorney comics as a kid, you cynical bastard."

Both men laughed.

"I confess, Maxie, I did read a few, but I'll bet you didn't miss a single episode when the 'Chief' and Miss Miller were on the radio. My grandfather loved that show. You know, before I was born he was an assistant DA under Tom Dewey, who was the original 'Mr. District Attorney'. We're all Democrats now, but Dewey was a god around our house. Even after he lost to Harry Truman in '48.

"Well, what do you have for me, Perry? Another surprise witness, a deathbed confession? Do I have to play Hamilton Burger again?"

"Okay, okay. I'll get to the point. This is bizarre and a lot more serious. You know that gang rape case you're prosecuting? The one where your vic has multiple personalities…?"

"How can I forget that one…hey, you're not defending one of those kids now, are you? If that's what this is about…"

"You know me better than that. See you in the morning. Off the record. 7:00 o'clock. The Bagel Basket, back booth."

"That's it? You get my curiosity up? You'll see me in the morning? You'll compromise my reputation being seen with you in public? You'll probably stick me with the check?"

"That's it. Want to know more, show up. 'Bye, Mr. DA." Maxie hung up before there was a reply.

The banter was a trademark of the respect and good humor existing between them. Barry Levine had picked up unsettling nuances from this conversation, however. Behind the wit, his worthiest courtroom opponent seemed anxious, impatient, almost abrupt, betraying an uncharacteristic urgency. And when was the last time they met for breakfast? How far off the record was this going to be?

In the men's room Maxie stared into the mirror, his face twisted with the lightning that flashed through his head. As the pang subsided, he said aloud as though sharing an aside with a friendly judge, "The brain may not feel pain, but it sure as hell can light up everything else." He popped two Oxycodone tabs and drew several deep breaths, propping himself against the sink top. Just two days ago he had received the news. He had a brain tumor. The good news was it wasn't malignant. The bad news was it was inoperable.

"Just one of those flukes." That's what Dr. Garner Kernchawk had said with a weak shrug of shoulders. The best Neuro-Oncologist in the Midwest and, Maxie would have wagered his next fee, the least empathetic. "It's going to continue to grow and where it's located, it will begin to affect your speech, your vision, your movement, then, one day, it will shut down your heart or your lungs. Like pulling out the wires on a switchboard until there are no more connections. There may be nothing we can do about it except ease your pain until it's over."

That was the clincher. Maxie had reacted, in words he himself might have used, like a pole-axed ox. "Doc. I appreciate your candor, but, damn, that's the coldest death sentence I've ever heard. And the only time I've personally been on the receiving end."

"Sorry if it came off that way. I'm not good at dissembling. You'll have to watch for other effects, too. Personality changes, memory impairment, muscle weakness, things like that. I'll schedule an appointment for next week to go over treatment options and give you more detail on what to expect." Anticipating the inevitable next question, Dr. Kernchawk went on. "If you want a second opinion I'll give you a list of three or four of the top Neuro-Oncologists in the country."

Maxie accepted the list, not knowing whether he would call, less sure exactly what he would do next. His indecision lay in the unexpectedness of the diagnosis, moreso the dark prognosis.

You hired Maxie Giuliano to defend you because, no matter how bad your case, with him you had hope. If he couldn't walk you, he could cut you a better deal. He was the master of reasonable doubt; methodical, seductive in his persuasiveness. If there was a chink in the prosecution's wall of proof, Maxie could chip it out enough to let light come through. Usually, that was enough. He had come to believe that he could affect the outcome of anything he chose to take on. When his time in the dock came around, however, he could not find a Maxie Giuliano to plead his case. His own mortality was the one charge he had never reckoned with.

Driving back to from the doctor's office, Maxie turned inward and to the past, reflecting on where he came from, now that it seemed he had nowhere to go.

Maxie's father returned to their second floor rooms above his mother's market each evening, gray with limestone powder, often with nicks and scrapes on his fingers, wounds that would heal as new scar tissue layered atop the old.

How gentle, he thought, might have been the caress of those knotty hands, the palms hard as old leather, had his father chosen tenderness. But those hands touched him only to discipline. The rock the old man cut showed more warmth than he, except when angered. Then curses would fly from his mouth like flaming rockets and the hands would flail like smashing sledges.

Nato and Daisy, his mother, slept in separate beds and hardly spoke. Maxie was his Mamma's boy, not because he wanted it, or necessarily because she did, but by default. It was a blessing to mother and son that the father grew more taciturn with age, avoiding and being avoided, until one bitter February evening when Maxie was just eighteen, Fortunato Giuliano coughed himself to sleep and did not wake up.

A week passed before the ground thawed enough to receive his body. A fellow mason fashioned the headstone, more out of respect than affection.

The figure was apt, if not art, inspired by Fortunato's unique style derived from the ancient traditions of his native land and rendered in the droll spirit of Calabrian folk culture. Atop the block one gnarled hand with comically exaggerated fingers and swollen knuckles held a sharp-tipped chisel; the other hand, wrapped around a fat wooden mallet, rose from a rough-hewn base, poised for eternity to complete the artisan's work.

Try as he might, Maxie could conjure no other image of his dead father, just those remorselessly hard, enduring hands, working the stone, making the perfect cut. Nor could he forget what his father had told him in a rare exchange just weeks before his death when they went to the shop where Fortunato finished a headstone to be delivered the next day. "When I carve a name on a stone, I am part of that person's life and it is part of me." To which now the grown son added aloud "and together you will be remembered in the hereafter because there will be no one left on earth to speak your name."

By her own choice Desideria Giuliano rested in death beside her husband, directly beneath the chisel's point.

CHAPTER TWENTY-FOUR

The cozy restaurant-bakery was the closest thing to a traditional Jewish delicatessen left in town. Here they at least knew the difference between Nova and belly lox and the half-sour tomatoes were authentic. You could ask for a "schmeer" and get cream cheese on your bagel; add "with sneakers" and get it to go. Levine was waiting in the booth farthest from the front door, his first cup of coffee awaiting a refill, the *Wall Street Journal* lying on the table folded back and over, taking up a minimum of space, to be read in quarter pages. He sensed more than saw Maxie coming and waved the waitress over without looking up.

Maxie slid across the vinyl bench just as she set a large mug of blistering black coffee in front of where he would be sitting. "Thanks, Julie. How about two scrambled with lox and onions and a plain bagel."

"Got fresh squeezed orange juice today, Mr. G."

"You squeeze it yourself?" He grinned at her, anticipating the answer.

"Marty bought it from the market last night."

"No thanks, dear, but I'm glad you asked."

Maxie nodded to his companion as the woman walked toward the counter. "Her brother got into a real jam about five years ago. A screwed up kid. Hijacking. I got him to flip on his accomplices and he was out in two years. She thinks I'm a genius. So do you, right?"

"Yes, and you walk on water, too. So, Maxie, what's so important we have to meet like this? I hope you have something good."

"Maybe good. Maybe not good. You got three guys for raping a woman called Hazel Bruning. Only, before they nailed her, she was Barbara, and she was coming on to one of them. Am I close?"

"Keep going..."

"So you got a hell of a problem. She's schizoid. Did they screw Barbara, who wanted it? Or did they force Hazel, who popped out in the middle of the party and told them to leave her alone, and they smacked her and held her down? How do you get past go?"

"You know the drill. Psychiatrists, hypnosis. This isn't the first multiple personality case in the world."

"It will make law here, though. And a conviction wouldn't hurt your image. I suppose that's why you're first chair on this, isn't it? So you have to get Hazel to testify she was raped and, *voila*, the defense brings out Barbara who says she was willing. Two for the price of one. Did they both know what the other one knew? Did Barbara get off while Hazel was screaming stop? Two people in one body. Maybe more?"

"Maxie, we're damned close to a serious ethical situation here. Where is this going?"

"Two days ago Nancy Featherwhite assigned me a case out of turn. She had her bailiff pull me from another courtroom. My client's name is Hazel Bruning, your Hazel Bruning. She's charged with performing oral sex on a fifteen-year-old boy whose parents want her head on a spit – no pun intended. My defense is that it wasn't Hazel, but Barbara, your Barbara."

"You're putting me on!"

"Not at all. We both have the same problem, but for you, it's worse. You have to take opposing positions in the two cases. The State Supremes say that Multiple Personality Disorder can avoid fault as a mental illness depending on a person's control over the personality shifts. I need to pin the crime on Barbara and show that she doesn't have control. Your ACA has to get a jury to believe that Barbara or Hazel and not the disease itself controlled the personality changes. By the way, a lot of judges think the whole idea of multiple personalities is psychobabble, so that throws more sand in the gears.

"You're going for multiple A felonies on first degree because of Hazel/Barbara's injuries. At worst you have a strong B felony case. Mine is a piddling D Felony. You've had that one kid up on rape before and got beat. So there's some pride on the line. You're plowing new ground. You have to show that Barbara's consent did not carry over to Hazel, that they really are distinct personalities controlled by the disease. Hazel, the good girl, is the real person, and Barbara is the oversexed switcheroo. And by the way, if my perp was Hazel, there goes your rape case!"

Maxie paused. "Have I confused you enough, yet?"

The Commonwealth's Attorney had begun by listening politely, half engaged, sipping his coffee. He expected to hear a snow job and was willing to be entertained. As the skilled advocate moved along, however, Levine's attention intensified, to the extent he showed irritation when Maxie stopped. "Keep talking. I'll let you know when I'm through listening."

"Okay, you say when.

"If Barbara could control the switch, you'll have a hell of a time convincing a jury that Hazel was subjected to forcible compulsion. As for the injuries, I'm guessing they beat Hazel because they got pissed off, thinking

Barbara was playing stupid games with them. Don't see any rape there, do you?

"I'm not telling you anything you haven't thought of. If Hazel's not your victim, then you're stuck with Barbara, and the physical injuries might not be enough to get you to the jury, let alone past it. You can win one and lose one on trial, depending on how the two judges and the two juries receive and process the evidence. You could win them both, or you could lose them both. One way or another I will take care of my client and that means I can win my case."

"Maxie, you have the damnedest knack for claiming victory before the game even begins."

"Not so. The ball is always in play and we both know the rules. It's just a game that allows unlimited substitutions. And while we're talking about substitutions, I'll bet you a dollar to a bialy we'll find more ladies inside when we pry the lid off Barbara's jar."

"You sure know how to ruin a man's day, don't you? Sometimes I'm not sure I don't hate your guts for making my job so difficult. I love a good challenge, but I'd rather put the bad guys away. So, other than making me miserable, what's the purpose of all this? You could have picked other ways to lecture me on how to do my job."

"This is no fun, Barry. But I have to do my best for my client. To tell the truth, I'm not exactly sure who my client is. Hazel is charged. She didn't do the deed. If we're right about MPD, she should walk. Then Barbara gets charged. Does she need a different lawyer? Would Barbara be subjected to double jeopardy because she shares the same body with Hazel? Hell, we couldn't write a movie script with these facts. No one would be willing to suspend their disbelief this far.

"You need for Hazel to be a rape victim. You need for Hazel/Barbara to be nuts. I want to plead Hazel, as Barbara, guilty but mentally ill and get her some treatment. This person - these people - I don't know what to call it - need help. Who's responsible, who's innocent? I'm not Solomon. This baby is already split. They've caused a lot of problems and without some intervention it'll get worse. We both know that. They get treatment; I've done right by my client, whoever she is. If Barbara/Hazel suffered from a mental illness, there's no consent, even though the defense can claim they didn't know she/they were mentally ill. You take your big rape case to trial and you've got a good chance to get convictions. Maybe plead it out and get some bad actors off the street for a while."

"Maxie, I'm beginning to think I'm the crazy one here. I have to believe all this crap before I can take it to court…"

"Not to worry. But I need the deal by next Monday."

"What's your hurry? You said you just got this case. And you've got that double murder down in Wheeler County… Whoa, we're not supposed to talk about that one, are we."

"Friend, for the first time in my life I'm thinking about cutting back. I'm not sure how many tough fights I have left in me. I'd like to do more fishing, take a trip - maybe to Italy. I've never been over there, where my people come from. And Susan's doing a great job with the Khalil boy's case. I haven't had enough fun. Maybe it's time." Maxie drifted into a dream-like silence.

He pulled a thread from his reverie. "Barry, how many people do you have inside of you? Ever wonder? The person you are in court, the one at dinner with your parents, in bed with your wife, on a vacation somewhere you've never been before and don't speak the language? Who are you when confronted by danger - a mugger on a dark street, a fatal illness? On stage, offstage, alone in the comfort of your favorite chair, who are you?"

In the twenty or so years of their acquaintance, Barry Levine had never experienced this detachment, the rambling banter, the bewilderment. It was, in fact, the opposite of the focused, crafty criminal defense attorney who had succeeded so brilliantly, the storyteller whose wit and timing were legendary. His concerns of the previous day were reinforced. *Who, indeed, are you, old friend?* The question lingered inside the prosecutor's head.

Maxie picked up the check and left a tip as large as the tab. He again projected the quiet dignity and intrinsic good humor for which he was known. His eyes were clear, his voice firm, his words spare.

The men parted with a handshake and an agreement to talk on Monday. One was unaware he had exposed his vulnerability. The other was embarrassed at having witnessed it and puzzled as to its source.

CHAPTER TWENTY-FIVE

Carnahan stood at the street corner, staring down a row of down-at-heel storefronts and seedy dives. The only new paint the buildings had seen in years was graffiti. Early evening shadows added an air of gloom to the neglect and dilapidation. The stench of urine and stale vomit assaulted his nose from doorways as he passed on the cracked and crumbling sidewalk, mixing with exhaust vapors from the street. It was a scene out of a 1940's black and white gangster film.

With Joseph trial approaching, Albert Thornburg was growing anxious about Matthew Patton's testimony. Patton had disappeared shortly after the little boys' funerals, returning from time to time to visit his wife and daughters, but ignoring subpoenas and messages to contact the sheriff's office. He was known to frequent the taverns in this district of Lexington, so Carnahan had set out to find him. Out of his jurisdiction, he wore civilian clothes. A half-zipped windbreaker concealed his nine-millimeter service pistol.

Cleve's Place was third on his list – the first two had turned up blanks. Carnahan stepped over the discarded wrapping of a fast food meal, stuck with a paste of mustard, ketchup and mayonnaise to the stoop. The front door was solid, a metal skin pierced by a single foot-square window, painted an ugly brown, chipped and splattered by weather and wear. It opened stiffly inward with the push of his hand. Stale, boozy air enveloped him, a mixture of fermented grain, tobacco smoke, disinfectant soap and human bodily excretions. His eyes squinched in the half-light of low watt bulbs hanging from mismatched chandeliers and wall mounts. The half-length mirror behind the bar managed only to compound the dreariness, obstructed as it was by smudgy discolorations and displays of liquor bottles, cigarettes, chewing gum, mints, snacks, condoms and assorted other sundries serving the incidental needs of the bar's patrons.

The barroom actually was two adjoining spaces divided by a five-foot wide floor to ceiling cutout and a shoulder-high partition wall over the top of which the bartender could keep an eye on what went on. An array of well-worn booths and Formica-topped tables lined the walls. Where not covered by vinyl, the wooden floors showed black with grime. The front-facing windows were shallow and bare, except for neon beer signs. A plate glass window faced the street from behind the bar. It was nearly filled by a translucent plastic sign displaying the name "Cleve's Place" in Old English script, with the name of a popular lager inscribed below.

How alike these places are, wherever you go, Carnahan reflected, including in his experience the joints he visited years before when a Cincinnati cop.

He perched on a stool near the front, his good foot braced against the tarnished brass rail laid along the full length of the bar's base. The bartender, a stout man of apparent middle age, was arched across the bar at the back of the room. He was sharing, as best Carnahan could make out, a coarse joke with two elderly customers who laughed over-loudly in the obsequious way of down-and-outers who had heard it before but hoped their enthusiasm would turn them a free drink.

"What'll it be, Pal?" the bartender said finally, pleasant enough but wary. He had sidled down to Carnahan's end of the bar, employing that oblique scuttle of tradespeople whose shallow workspace demands they move efficiently to face someone whose money they hope they soon will be taking.

"Miller draft - mug."

In a single swing of his left arm, the barman lifted a glass mug from beneath the counter, held it under the tap to be filled and placed it on the bar in front of the deputy. "That'll be a buck two bits." Stubby fumbled in his pocket for some change and slapped down a single and a quarter, which were efficiently scooped up and dropped into the cash drawer.

Carnahan got to his business before the man could move away. "I'm looking for someone. He may be a customer of yours, Matthew Patton." He pulled a photograph from a jacket pocket and held it up.

"You a bill collector or a cop? You got to be one or the other. You sure as hell ain't here for happy hour."

"My name is Dale Carnahan. I'm a deputy sheriff from over in Wheeler County. Looking for a witness." He unclipped the badge from his belt and set it on the bar.

"He's not in any trouble? This Patton fella?"

"No. His little boy was killed - murdered - and we need him to testify at the trial. It starts in a few weeks."

The bartender hesitated, then softened his tone. "Yeah, I know Matthew, and he told me some about his boy and his sister's kid being found dead. He was drinking hard and didn't make a lot of sense. He comes in here every once in a while. I haven't seen him lately, though."

"Can you tell me where I can find him? Where he stays?"

"Sure can't. I just know he's from Tackbottom, same as his daddy and all his people. I used to have some kinfolk over there. Boggses. I'm Cleve Boggs. This is my place."

Carnahan strayed from the script, his curiosity aroused. Rebecca had told him about her father's death in a bar fight and the case being unsolved. She had never been happy that the Lexington police dropped their investigation so soon. His killer was long gone and they told her in so many words the death of an old drunk was not worth their effort.

"You knew his father, Dander Patton?"

"Sure did. He was sitting over there in that corner just before he was killed. Old Dander was some kind of a hell raiser. He knew he could come over here and I'd look after him, though. Did, too. Except one time." Boggs's voice trailed off as his eyes drifted from Stubby's face to an empty table across the room.

"Did you see what happened?"

"Not really. Told the cops everything I knew. Got 'em the names of some of the others…regulars… who was here that night. Didn't seem to make any difference, though. They just gave up. Figured he was just a mean old wino who got what he asked for. May be. But I don't believe it. He was ornery as sin and foul-mouth as they come. But he was a coward down deep. Woulda run from a real fight."

"I wonder. What did you see?" Carnahan shifted on the stool, resting his forearms on the bar top, concentrating on the bartender, who seemed eager to tell the story.

"Ol' Dander come in about eleven of the evening with some woman. Younger, better looking than most I seen him with before. No prize, mind you, but I figured she was just a higher priced whore. I don't let them hustle in here but if a gent brings one in I let 'em stay. Well, he bought a couple rounds and she pulled on him to go. They both was kinda high. He come over to the bar to settle up. He showed me a roll of bills. Said he was gonna have a big time. Then him and her left outa here."

"You know where they were going?"

"Let me take care of Ollie here." One of the old men at the end of the bar held up an empty mug. Boggs drew a fresh draft, carried it down and stayed a few minutes. Carnahan guessed he was the subject of discussion.

Boggs returned, poured himself a shot of vodka, downed it in a single swallow, and went on. "Let's see. Where'd he go? No. Didn't pay any mind. Business was kind of light, about like now, so I called last round and started cleaning up. Folks began clearing out. I was shutting off the lights in the other room when Jernie Miller, one of my regulars, ran back in and hollered 'There's a dead man outside!' 'Course I jumped up and ran out the door.

"There was poor old Patton, laying on his face in the doorway next door...the pawn shop...blood running across the sidewalk. I called the police right away. They picked up a knife next to his body. One of the cops told me later it must of been Dander's because it didn't have no blood on it and wasn't what killed him. Said his money was gone, too.

"One of the boys said he heard some loud talking before Jernie found the body, looked outside..." Boggs pointed at the windows in the far room. "...said some fella and Dander was arguing, like maybe over the woman. But there was no one there when I got outside, just Patton."

Stubby weighed whether to leave well enough alone. This was, after all, not what he came for. And what happened to Dander Patton was officially none of his business. He couldn't resist asking another question, however. "You think he was set up, killed for that wad of money?"

Growing visibly uncomfortable with what was becoming a full-blown interrogation, Boggs turned surly. "Look, Deputy Dale whatever-your-name-is, I put all this out of mind a long time ago. You came looking for Matthew. I don't know where the hell he is. His daddy was a friend of mine. If you're looking to find who murdered him, that's fine. If you're just nosy, get the hell outa my place!"

Carnahan couldn't answer. He didn't know what his motives were. He smiled and stood to go. "Thanks. I've come to know the family since the little boys were murdered. I care about what happens. I would appreciate if you hear from Matthew you call me or the prosecuting attorney. He can help us get at least one killer." He scribbled Thornburg's name and toll free number on the back of his card and handed it to the barman. "As for Dander, I think his daughter would like to know what happened. Maybe I can help, maybe I can't."

Boggs took the card, looked at the print and turned it over. "Sure. I see him, I'll let you know." He closed his eyes and drew a long breath. "Could of been the money; could of been the woman. Never made sense to me Dander having to die. That kind of hullabaloo over money and floozies happens all the time down here. People get beat up and cut, sometimes shot, but hardly nobody gets killed." He hesitated, then leaned into Carnahan's ear. "Dander told me something else when he paid up. I never told nobody. Didn't seem important then. Said he 'caught the old stud covering a filly' and it was gonna pay off. I don't have no idea what it means, but maybe you can figure it out."

Darkness had come. The bronze glow of street lamps did nothing to relieve the grimness of the block. Stubby stopped on the sidewalk in front of the pawnshop. His detective's mind reconstructed the scene where a man had been stabbed to death six years earlier and chalked a mental outline of the corpse as it lay in a bloody pool. Dander Patton was a worthless scoundrel by most accounts, but his daughter deserved something to help make sense of the tragedies that marred her young life. Part of Dale Carnahan wanted to give Rebecca that something but no, this was something he would not pursue. It really was none of his business.

CHAPTER TWENTY-SIX

Joseph asked Susan if he could get a fair trial in Wheeler County.

The question, posed matter-of-factly during a prep session in Jock Dowd's office to discuss the prosecution's case, demanded more than a glib answer. He asked it at a time when he had come to believe she respected his intelligence and total involvement in his defense. He wanted details, facts, and honest, useful advice. She started to explain in terms meant to reassure and comfort him.

"You can count on Maxie and me to make sure you do," she said. "A lot goes into making sure your rights are protected."

He motioned her to stop. "Like, don't treat me like some ignorant shoplifter or druggie. Tell me about the system and how I can expect it to work – for and against me. Okay?"

Susan realized she dared not ad lib an answer. "Wait here a minute. I'll get you something," she said and left the conference room.

She returned a few minutes later, three freshly printed sheets of paper in hand. "This is the text of a talk I gave about a year ago to a citizens' group concerned that judges and juries might be letting guilty criminals go free. I decided to give them a primer on our jury system. I put this together from a lot of sources. Read it and then I'll answer your questions."

Joseph took the papers and began reading.

Citizen juries date from ancient times.

Our jury system comes down from the Great Charter of King John of England in 1215. You probably recognize it as 'Magna Carta.' It says 'No freeman shall be seized, or imprisoned, or dispossessed, or outlawed, or in any way destroyed; nor will we condemn him, nor will we commit him to prison, excepting by the legal judgement of his peers, or by the laws of the land.' The word jury derives from the French 'jure', to swear. The idea and the system came to us from Great Britain when the American colonies were settled. We have refined it over time, written it into our federal and state constitutions and our laws.

Joseph tossed the sheets onto the table and glared at Susan. "I don't give a rat's ass about King John. What's going to happen to me?"

The young attorney stared back, red faced. He was right. She had treated him as a pupil, not as a client in jeopardy of being found guilty of aggravated murder by twelve randomly chosen people. She needed for him to understand what it meant in the real, not abstract, world. She had twice misjudged Joseph. She would try to get it right this time.

She came around the table, sat next to him and faced him, resisting the urge to reach out and hold his hands.

"Look, Joseph, I'm sorry. It seems every time I try to help you I just make things worse. You are not a typical client, if there is such a thing. Sometimes I treat you like a sixteen-year-old kid then over-correct and appeal to your intelligence." She carefully weighed her next words. "You want to be in charge of your defense. That's understandable. But you have to trust Maxie and me to help you through this. The system is the system, whether you or we like it or not..."

Joseph leaned toward Susan, interrupting. "I don't like the system and I don't like being talked down to."

His tone was matter of fact, free of overt hostility, but the message was clear and commanding.

Susan had thought herself beyond intimidation by a client. Maxie had early impressed on her the importance of controlling the relationship while at the same time actively engaging the client in his or her defense. It was a balancing act, especially in their chosen area of the law. It made no difference whether the charge was petty theft or murder or multi-million dollar securities fraud, the survival instinct was the same. The more intelligent or highly educated the person, the more difficult was the task.

"Let me try again. Let's have a conversation about what it means to have a fair trial. Okay?"

The boy broke eye contact and sat back in his chair. Obviously still skeptical, he seemed willing to give her another go at it. His murder trial was a game Joseph had every intention to win. And part of winning was knowing the rules. If he didn't like their rules, he would substitute his own. After all, that's what he had always done. He would let her explain the rules.

"You are entitled to a trial by a jury of your peers – that's basically what it means to have a fair trial."

Joseph cocked his head in her direction and seemed about to speak. Susan held her breath. How had she messed up this time? He said nothing and she continued.

"Peers means equals. Today it means trial by a jury of your fellow citizens."

"You mean those clods from Wheeler County? How can you believe they are my equals?" Joseph sat at the edge of his seat, angling his bulk toward the door.

"I said this would be a conversation. That means I don't do all the talking. It also means we can agree at least to listen to each other. Can we give that a try? If it doesn't work, then maybe I'm not the right lawyer for you and we'll let you and Maxie have this talk." It was a gamble. Maxie would be quicker than she to decide whether they could be effective. He taught her early on if you can't help the client, don't be his lawyer, no matter what it costs you.

Joseph flashed a faint, impatient smile – his first of the session – and waved her to continue. He dropped his gaze to the long, stockinged legs tucked under her chair. At this point, Joseph was more interested in Susan's body than her words.

"The people who sit on a jury are not supposed to favor any party and will render judgment only after the trial, considering all the evidence. We know, though, in the real world each juror comes with built-in prejudices. They're people you would see on the street or meet in daily life."

"Like those farmers and hillbillies, those people off the street who are nothing like me and probably don't have anything better to do, are going to decide whether I committed murder? How fair is that, lady? How do you and Super Mario get me there?"

"Well, Joseph, look at it this way. The first juries in England were picked because they were not impartial. The more they knew about what happened the more likely they would be selected. Under that system, the little boys' parents would be right up there. Go figure."

"Yeah, thank God this isn't Merry Old England. The thought of those Tackers after my blood is not funny. I hear they think I'm the devil. These are the same people who burned witches at the stake."

Susan chose not to argue. She needed to keep him engaged. Seeing where his eyes had roamed, she turned away and smoothed her skirt, covering her thighs.

"The potential jurors will have to answer a lot of personal questions before they can be chosen. Based on their answers we may disqualify them for cause, such as an obvious bias, and some of them without any cause at all. Maxie's the best at picking a jury. And your Uncle Jock will help us. During the trial the judge will rule on the law and instruct the jury on the law before they begin deliberations."

"You mean Judge Benny, the guy who already hates my guts! He's gonna follow the law?"

It had been impossible to keep from Joseph Judge Willards' reputation for playing politics and challenging lawyers to take his questionable rulings to the Court of Appeals. Despite his having caved to Jasper Dowd's pressure and granting bail, this judge clearly would bend in the wind, which blew decidedly away from Joseph Khalil.

"Well, if we can convince the jury that you're not guilty, he can't throw out the verdict."

"Jeez, that sounds like a really big 'if'."

"I can't make this anything but what it is, Joseph."

"And you're telling me that this is going to be fair and impartial? All I hear is how screwed I am. And for Christ's sake, don't tell me again how good you and your boss are!"

Whatever else Susan might have wanted to say she decided would only make things worse. This client was beyond reassurance and his trust was worn thin.

A plan was forming in Joseph's mind as he prepared to leave - a plan to get a verdict on his terms. If he could fight battles, create and recreate himself in games and made up worlds, why could he not also have a trial in a community of his choosing, in front of a jury of his peers?

CHAPTER TWENTY-SEVEN

Jock Dowd's voice through the phone cranked a few decibels and a half octave higher than usual.

"Maxie, Joseph's gone! He slipped his electronic monitor and took off last night! Besides the panic Jeannie Ann and Eddie are in, we'll have hell to pay with Bennie Willards. He's issued a bench warrant and his clerk says he wants you, Susan and me in front of him tomorrow morning at ten."

Maxie received the unwelcome report without obvious alarm. "Okay, Jock, draw a breath and calm down. This isn't the first scared kid who's bolted when trial got close. He's likely not gone very far. He'll be in touch with us or his parents within 24 hours. About the worst will happen is that Willards will lock him up. We can live with that..."

"Yeah, but can Joseph? Jock interrupted.

"...it just makes our job harder. This gets out..."

"And it sure as hell will..."

"This gets out and..."

"...everybody in the county and across the state, probably the whole darn country, will know about this by dark."

"Look, Susan's over in Lexington. I'll get word to her. I'm in trial here, a major fraud case, so I doubt I can be there. You two will have to handle it."

"Benny'll really be hacked, Maxie."

"Yeah, but he's not likely to get into a pissing contest with a U. S. District Court Judge. He'll blow off steam, say a few choice words about the self-important Mr. 'Joo-lee-ah-noh' and do whatever he's going to do. We just need to be ready."

"Tell Susan to meet me at Jeannie Ann's as soon as she can; I'll wait on her. I'm sure the place is already covered up with cops."

The handset was not yet cradled when Willie Mae stuck her head in her boss's door. "Susan's on the horn. Seems she's got some bad news..."

Maxie blew a long, weary, old man's sigh, then put the receiver to his ear. "How'd you hear, girl?"

"What? You mean you already know about Joseph Khalil? I just got off the phone with Thornburg. He all but accused me of setting it up and helping the boy get away. I don't know what the hell is going on..."

"But you know about being in front of Bennie Willards in the morning. I won't be there."

Susan caught herself, suppressing the urge to explode into the phone. "You're letting me face the music all by myself? I don't have any idea what to expect – or what to say. I've never had a bail jumper with this much at stake before. And there's enough shit in this game already!"

"Young lady, grow up!" The tone was harsh. "Tonight you find out all you can about what happened. Jock'll be looking for you at Doctor Khalil's house quick as you can get over there. Tomorrow morning, you tell Judge Willards what you know that's not privileged. You don't apologize. It isn't your fault Joseph skipped. Benny'll do most of the talking. You stand there and take it as calmly as you can. He'll be nasty and rude. But you take it. Behind all the bluster, he needs to know that you appreciate the gravity of what has happened and that you'll be professional about the consequences."

"That's a good word," Susan said. "Consequences. What's that mean?"

"It means he won't lock you up but he can make our lives miserable. He went out on a limb and granted bail. I still don't understand why. He could have kept the kid locked up and we couldn't have done much about it. We've had our bite at that apple and we can't expect a damn thing more. He'll be pissed because now all those people who bitched about what he did will be vindicated and no judge, let alone Bennie Willards, likes the taste of crow feathers. He'll revoke bail and put every peace officer in the country on the road looking for Joseph. And whatever our defense would have been we now have to deal with the reasons an innocent person would skip."

"And I'm supposed to just stand there and take it?"

"Just remember what I told you about not aggravating Thornburg because I didn't want him behaving erratically. Same for the judge. Let him be the judge. That way he's predictable. He's never going to be on our side, but we can't have him taking this personally. Our edge is that we let him be who he is. Do you understand? I don't want to take any more risks than we have to. And get your detective hat on. We need to find the boy before the court does. You *gabish*?"

Susan held her tongue, absorbing Maxie's meaning. The words were the sternest yet in their association — there was good cause and this was the right time — but an odd irritability infected them. Even to the point of mocking her penchant for peppering her conversation with fractured movie Mafia dialogue.

"I'll take care of it, Mr. G." She acquiesced with just the right amount of subservience and a sincere, if forced, lilt in her voice.

"Thanks. Call me about 4:30 tomorrow. Let me know what happened. And good luck. You'll do just fine," he said, his tone closer to normal.

The call ended without a formal good-bye. Neither of them felt the need.

Maxie turned to the witness outline spread across his desk. He held his head between thick, clammy palms, pressing at the temples to ease the fire that smoldered in his head and occasionally spiked into flame.

Susan had been preparing for the final pretrial conference when Thornburg called. His tone was best described as a blend of delight and anger. Joseph's disappearance strengthened the Commonwealth's case but created other potential complications, including delay of trial. She had let Thornburg spout and sputter. Accustomed as she was to restraint in dealing with her adversary, especially since the talk with Maxie on their first visit to Parkersburg, Thornburg's assault stretched her resolve nearly to breaking.

She regretted venting on Maxie.

CHAPTER TWENTY-EIGHT

Susan thought ahead to the next day's hearing with Thornburg and Judge Willards as she drove from Lexington to the Khalil home in Wheeler County. It would certainly be unpleasant; Jock would buffer the impact, but she would have to swallow most of the vitriol the judge and prosecutor would surely spew at her - for her own alleged misdeeds and for the absence of esteemed lead counsel.

"Let him be himself." Isn't that what Maxie had said about Bennie Willards? *"He'll never be on our side, anyway."*

Susan envied the deference shown Maxie by nearly all the sitting judges. He had earned it over time by the force of his conduct both in and out of the courtroom. His edge was the respect they had for integrity and honest advocacy. His clients enjoyed a priceless benefit because he rarely overstated a position and could be counted on to deliver on any promise to the court — or have an ironclad reason if he did not.

With no hope of gaining Judge Willards' favor, she just might be able to hold him at bay by absorbing his best shot and keeping her own dignity.

Susan recalled vividly the session in Maxie's office not long after she joined his firm. She had endured the disdain of a senior judge who had exhibited little tolerance for her inexperience in a courtroom and seemed offended by both her age and her gender. Frustrated and more than a little depressed, Susan had dropped by Maxie's office late in the day, needing his perspective. He had listened patiently, letting her get it all out.

"How do you win the respect of a judge? How do you earn the benefit of his considerable discretion? You need to know about my very first trial in the old Police Court.

"My first client, my first solo representation, was an old character from the Hay Market, Charles Buzhardt - Chollie Buzz - a wino and petty thief who never really caused any harm. Most of the people on Jefferson Street tolerated him and overlooked his frailties, like you might treat a stray dog that was lazy and never minded what you said to him — and every once in a while peed on your leg – but endeared himself anyway."

Susan had smiled with understanding, picturing the man without knowing any of his physical characteristics.

"Anyway, one day he was mooching around Annie Pelacutis's little produce store. She must have been in a bad mood because she chased him out with a broom and let him have shot of broken English insults to his ancestry and personal hygiene." Maxie stood, lustily swinging an invisible broom and stalking around the office, and, in heavily accented falsetto, he mimicked the scene.

"'You no good sunamabitch, you stinkin' bagashit, you get you bastard ass outa my store. I call Murphy; he lock you up!' Murphy was the beat cop.

"Well, you could say just about anything to Chollie, just about any time, and he'd just shrug it off and shuffle on down the street. For some reason, he was in just as foul a mood as Annie that day. He stopped on the sidewalk, looking gimlet-eyed at the three hundred pound woman railing at him and waving a bunch of wet straw in his face. Without uttering a word, he kicked out with a scrawny leg and knocked over the display of vegetables—including lots of ripe tomatoes—that lined the storefront. When the stuff hit the pavement, Chollie Buzz went into this crazy dance and mashed everything underfoot, creating the damnedest mess you ever saw and sending Annie P. into apoplexy. She charged at him screaming bloody murder and took a hard swing at the old man's head with the broom. He ducked. She missed and whirled around off balance, right in the middle of Chollie's fresh tomato sauce. Her big backside hit the concrete — splat! — and stuck there."

Maxie reenacted the encounter with a mime's precision and a comic's timing. Tears streamed down his young associate's cheeks. Several of the office staff had gathered at the office door and, though many of them had seen this routine before, they never tired of enjoying their boss in his lighter moments. There was no question they laughed with him and not at him, so great was his skill and so deep their admiration of him.

"Murphy heard the commotion and huffed up the block just in time to get splattered when Annie hit the deck. He tried to stop, but his momentum and the slimy sidewalk carried him right into Chollie, still stomping away with both feet. The cop and the wino did the two-step for a few seconds, then joined the old woman on the ground.

"So I got the case. There wasn't any money in it, but my mother saw it all and told me I needed to help out old 'Chollie Booz', because he entertained everybody that day, and besides, 'That Annie, she got no class. You gotta give the regulars something to keep 'em alive. They don' hurt nobody.' Mamma usually justified her acts of charity by letting the derelicts wash a window, sweep the sidewalk, carry out garbage — something to satisfy herself that they had earned a coin or a piece of fruit — and that it was not just a handout. She had lived through the Depression and the War and knew first hand about hardship.

166

"Annie pushed it, so they brought Chollie up on Breach of the Peace. He spent just enough time in jail to get cleaned up and we had to go in front of the judge. I thought Charlie ought to plead out and get 30 days, which I thought wouldn't hurt him, anyway. I told the geezer so. Big mistake. I learned then and there not to take a client's incarceration lightly. What I thought didn't make a damn bit of difference to him. He didn't think he did anything wrong and he wasn't going to spend one minute locked up he didn't have to. Besides, this wasn't his first time in court — far from it. So I had my first trial.

"Judge Howard Hogaboom sat on the bench. He was a rough piece of work and didn't have much sympathy for criminals. There wasn't any such thing as a close case with "The Boomer". Anywhere near the line and you were guilty. He knew the chances of an appeal to Circuit Court were slim to none, so he rode defendants and their lawyers pretty hard. His Honor knew I hadn't tried a case before, but he had seen me around when I clerked for Murray Schepper while I was in law school. And he used to shop down on Jefferson Street and stopped at Mamma's place every once in awhile. Whenever I saw him I would say something polite — you know that's the way I was brought up. He was sort of gruff, though, and I never knew what kind of mood he was in. When I said I was ready for trial, he looked down at me — I felt like a mouse in a corner — and smiled like he was the cat who couldn't wait to grab me.

"'Mr. Giuliano,' he said, 'Why are you trying this case? You'll do us all a favor if you just enter a plea. I'll give ol' Chollie 30 days to dry him out with credit for time served and we can all go back to important things.' I was so scared I thought I'd wet my pants.

"'S' Sir... Your Honor,' I said, 'I have discussed the matter with my client and he wants a trial. I have to honor his wishes.' Boy, was I naive. The other lawyers waiting their turns and the hangers on in the courtroom snickered or laughed out loud. To my surprise, the Judge banged his gavel and told them to shut up or he'd put them out. 'The boy wants a trial and by God, he's going to get a trial.' The hungry smile on his lips had straightened to a grim line that said 'Okay, it's your funeral. Let's get on with it.'

"I really puckered up then. He was going to teach me a lesson.

"The prosecutor from the City Attorney's office was Tony Moore, an okay guy who did this for a living and needed only to go through the motions to get a quick conviction when someone insisted on a trial. He put on Annie and Murphy. They testified about like I described it. Annie had cooled off but still wanted her pound of flesh. Murphy went by the book. Almost by rote, just like you've noticed most cops testify. I got nowhere with cross-examination; it seemed like all I did was dig the hole deeper. I sure as hell wasn't going to call my client to the stand.

"When Tony rested the prosecution's case, I realized he never asked either witness whether the offense occurred in Louisville, Jefferson County, Kentucky. I knew that the City had to prove the crime was committed inside the city limits. I guessed maybe the Judge would infer it just by knowing that the 300 block of East Jefferson Street was in Louisville. It was slim as hell, but I stood on my hind legs and in my most cocksure voice moved to dismiss the charge and explained why. Moore jumped to his feet and moved to reopen. He realized his careless mistake and took for granted it could easily be rectified.

"The Boomer looked at Tony, then at me, then back and forth again, silent as a statue. He pulled at his jowls, the faintest glimmer of a grin lifting the corners of his mouth. I was dead. I knew it. He'd let the question be asked and Chollie Buzz would get jail time and I'd have fallen on my ass, just like Annie Pelacutis. I shrank six inches I couldn't spare waiting for the inevitable.

"'Case dismissed! Mr. Moore, next time prove venue.' Tony's jaw dropped to his knees.

"I straightened up and beamed with pride and astonishment. I had won my first case!

"Judge Hogaboom turned to me. 'As for you, Mister Giuliano, you stayed awake. Good for you and your client. This time! But don't bring these crap cases in front of me again! Understand?'

"I swallowed hard. 'Yes, your Honor,' I answered meekly, almost obediently. I guess I meant it then, but you have to learn not to let a judge intimidate you, else you won't be worth a damn to your client.

"No one could figure why I got the break. I was a hero around the Courthouse. And maybe it led to business that I wouldn't have got otherwise. The judge could have let the proof in. You never know. But it seems my reputation as a winner started that day. In fact, I got my name in the afternoon paper the next day. A beat reporter - just a kid - happened to be hanging around, waiting for a traffic case involving one of the Aldermen. He wrote a little piece that showed up on page three of the second section. The headline read 'Rookie Lawyer Wins First Case'; it took up as much space as the article. I had it framed. It's around here somewhere."

Maxie slumped in his chair. The early hilarity had subsided. The crowd had dispersed and Susan sat relaxed and calm, her mood much improved.

"But you found out why he helped you?"

"No. I never asked and, though we became good friends over the years and I had other cases in front of him after he moved up to Circuit Court, we never mentioned that one. Doing what you think is right at the time and being ready to take your licks is usually worth it. People know when you're screwing them over. Maybe The Boomer just bought that I was doing what I believed I ought to and it caused him to do the same. We won't ever know. He died about eight years ago. Cancer of the throat. Wasted away to nothing. I visited him in the hospice the day before he went."

'And the reporter...?"

"He's still around. You know him. Griggsbie."

A green road sign overhead announced the exit to Parkersburg. Susan turned her attention to the immediate challenge of dealing with Eddie and Jeannie Ann Khalil and trying to get Joseph back before the law did. His flight had weakened her belief in his innocence, but she could not let that influence what she would have to do in the coming days. The thought nagged her that something she had said or done in the past few days had triggered his flight. But he seemed so involved, so aware. Maybe too aware!

CHAPTER TWENTY-NINE

Griggsbie showed up late the same day Maxie found out about Joseph Khalil's escape. The lawyer was digging through the pleadings of another case, preparing for his U.S. District Court appearance the next day.

"How do I write it, Maxie? Broad strokes or bullet points?"

"Damn, that was quick! Slow news day?"

Griggsbie lounged against the door jamb, hands thrust deep in the pockets of baggy khakis, one loafered foot firm on the floor, the heel of the other dug into the carpet, sole poised. An unlit cigarette – a sterile vestige of his former three pack a day habit – hung from a corner of his mouth, the downward angle abetted by a scowl.

"You look like a bad imitation of a B movie version of a crime reporter. The only thing missing is the scruffy porkpie hat. Get your sorry ass in here and into that chair!" Maxie half stood and pointed at the scarred leather chair opposite him, grinning. "And what's this 'how' stuff? I never tell you how to write, just what."

The lawyer's bluff levity did not take. Griggsbie's dour expression didn't change even as he plopped into the chair and leaned forward. He said nothing, just looked sadly into his old pal's eyes. Maxie was puzzled, off guard. The reporter was stonewalling him, expecting him to fill the silence. It was an interrogator's trick that could be more effective than a clever question. Griggsbie had always been a sourball and a skeptic, but now his manner bordered on rudeness.

Maxie obliged. "You here to ding me for that kid's hotfooting it? You want to talk about this computer game stuff?"

Griggsbie's eyes said it was not just about the case.

"Maxie, you worthless sonofabitch, the buzz is you're losing your touch. The brass at the paper, who never liked you anyway, love it that you're not invincible. They sent me to do a feature story, figure I'll give it a unique perspective, seeing's how I've covered your career since you won your first case." He spurted the words in a single breath, then braked as though he were about to hit a wall. He inhaled sharply, relaxed, exhaled.

"Feature, my Anglo-Saxon ass," he said, his voice low and gritty, "they want me to write your freaking obituary."

Maxie's expression didn't change. Even in front of this man who knew him better than anyone, who had been privy to some of his deepest secrets, he was capable of showing the poker face, the avuncular smile that hid whatever went on behind his deep brown eyes. He did not telegraph his moves and did not let you know when he was hurt.

"I'll spare you the Mark Twain quote, Griggsbie. But I'm not quite ready to check out." His reply was dry and matter-of-fact, bereft of the wit and humor that ordinarily laced his speech. That alone was enough to tip the reporter to the seriousness of what must be ailing his friend.

"Okay, you old bastard, you know I'm off the record until you say the word, but you're not as good at fooling people as you think you are. I've been around you so long I can tell how many cups of coffee you had this morning and whether you had beef or chicken for dinner last night. I've fished with you and I've watched you in a hundred trials. I can tell when you're letting the line play out and when you're ready to set the hook. Most people want to be conned, they can't help themselves, and you're the best. Hell, society is lucky you picked this side of the law." Griggsbie punctuated his words with a wave of the arm describing the lawyer's office.

"You'd be public enemy number one if you were on the other side. But you'd damn well better come clean with me or you'll be reading what somebody else wants me to say. You haven't been the same these past few days. And yeah, it does have something to do with this Khalil boy's getting away and whether you've lost your touch or your ethics...but that's not all." He broke off, aware that he had taken one step too far.

Trying to salvage the visit, Griggsbie tossed a softball. "Look, Maxie, tell me how you decided to become a lawyer. I've never asked you that before. We can go from there."

"No, you haven't. I can guess why now. What good is Omega without the Alpha?

"When did I decide to become a lawyer? That's easy. When I was about fifteen years old, after the War. When I sat in on my first sit-down."

"Which is...?"

"Italian justice, a kind of tribal court. A respected man of the community would hear grievances, try to steer the parties to resolve their differences and, if necessary, decide for them. His decision was more powerful than a judge's order. Compliance was immediate and mandatory. No appeals, no stays. Disobedience could bring unpleasant consequences, but I never knew of anybody who did not go along."

"I thought that was just a 'Mafia' thing. You know, peacemaking, dividing turf."

"Shame on you, Griggsbie. Of all people, an old courthouse hound like you should know better. You don't have to be a Bonanno or Giancana or Gotti. All issues are big to the people they involve and a sit-down was in many ways more likely to yield the right result than a court. Unfortunately, it served a culture that's disappearing. You know, sometimes I choose bench trials just because I have a judge and a prosecutor who are willing to seek a right result. We relax some of the rules. It's a risk, because my client loses the protections of a jury trial but it can be just as fair."

"Maxie, you're confusing me…"

"That's a first!"

"No, I'm serious. You said this sit-down thing led you to practice law. The operative principle in your world is 'let justice be done'. But you describe this sit-down as producing 'right' outcomes. I think there's a difference."

"Yeah. Weird, isn't it? Getting justice and doing the right thing aren't exactly the same, are they? Let's just say I fell in love with the process. The awesome power of the law. What comes out in the end, we can call that justice. Of course, I didn't understand all this at the time and I sure as hell couldn't articulate it."

The lawyer leaned backward, reflective, assembling the pieces of the tale he was about to tell.

"My mother's kitchen table became a gathering place for meals, card games, my homework – whatever – and Uncle Pete's sit-downs. A dark oak circle surrounded by mismatched wooden chairs. Mamma cooked and served the food, and cleaned up after everyone, but she had no part in what I call the society of the table. I took for granted the power of my gender and the weakness of hers. I respected her as my mother, a good Catholic. Subservience went against her nature and sense that in America it should not be this way. But she played her role well and without complaint for many years."

Griggsbie held up an interrupting hand. "Whoa, pardner, sounds like Daisy did the hard work and you're just now giving her the credit she deserved."

"It is strange how I'm just now tying together the sit-down and my mother. Until today, I don't think I ever consciously connected becoming a lawyer and my feelings about Mamma."

The moment of epiphany past, Maxie resumed the telling of his initiation into the administration of justice, such as it was then, and a far distance from where he found himself now.

"Anyway, Carlo Greco, one of the early immigrants from Sicily, had a produce business. He saved his money and bought property. His first purchase was the storefront where he ran his business, then the 25 front feet next to it. He rented it to another Sicilian, Franco Ciccolini, who opened a butcher shop and moved his family into the second floor.

"Less than a year later, Greco wanted to expand, so he went next door and told Ciccolini he had thirty days to get out. He could continue to live upstairs at half the rent. When Chico protested, Greco threatened to have the sheriff evict him. After all, they had no written lease. With prosperity he was adopting the ways of the *'Mrigani.'*"

Maxie chuckled, looked sheepishly at Griggsbie. "Whoops, does that sound too *Mafioso*? Anyway, that was unheard of. No one set the law on a *goombah*.

"So Ciccolini asked for a sit-down. At first, Greco resisted, but my father, who played *bocce ball* and cards with them both, urged him to honor the call.

"You have to understand. They came from a place where the courts and police, the army – all government agencies – were distrusted. For good reason. They favored the wealthy, the bosses, the landowners, the politicians. Our people were the poor, the laborers, the tenants. You had your family, your village and the Church. In this country, it seemed the same. The police and judges could not be relied upon to give justice to Italian immigrants so it had to come from within the community. Even the Catholic Church was suspect. It was run by the Irish and the Germans who treated Italians like pagan intruders. But that, as they say, is another story.

"It was a weekday evening, after supper. Uncle Pete came in first. He brought a jug of homemade red wine and plopped it in the middle of the table. 'To ease the way', I recall he said. Pete was in the 'distribution' business and could be relied on to get hold of just about anything - even during the War when stuff was rationed. And he made book..."

"...Like a whole slew of your clients," Griggsbie threw in.

Maxie nodded agreement. "Only in those days handbooks were tolerated as long as it didn't get violent and the betting was on the up and up. Hell, Uncle Pete was damn near benevolent, although he knew how to collect from a deadbeat if he had to. Besides, half his customers were judges, cops and public officials. He didn't get out of the business until the syndicate horned in and wanted him to be their man. Getting mobbed up wasn't something this town was going to accept."

"How was he related to you? Why 'Uncle' Pete?"

"He was supposed to have been related to my mother through her mother. As far as anyone knew, he was blood kin and our fierce protector. Mamma was born in New York in 1913, about six months after her mother and father arrived here from Sicily. They died in the big influenza epidemic in 1918 and she lived for a while with a Sicilian family willing to take in the orphan girl. I think they treated her pretty badly, though, more as a servant. When she turned fourteen and became uncontrollable, the family sent her here to live with Uncle Pete's mother. That's the best story I've ever been able to get, and I'm stuck with it."

The reporter squelched a smile. "Back to the sit-down, Maxie. I need to keep my mouth shut."

"Ciccolini and Greco came up the stairs together. Both had scowls on their faces and avoided looking at each other. Chico shuffled through the doorway, hat clutched in hands like a beggar. Carlo stomped indignantly across the floor, unable to hide his anger, as sure of his righteousness as a Baptist preacher. Uncle Pete and Pappa passed pleasantries with both men, each in his way trying to lighten the mood.

"'Mario, put coal in the stove', Pappa said. I hadn't noticed it was particularly cool, but I shoveled a few lumps from the scuttle into the cast iron potbelly that heated the kitchen. Pappa sat opposite Pete. I stoked the stove and started to go to my room. 'Boy,' he called and tilted his chin toward the chair beside him. 'You stay here.' Uncle Pete nodded and winked at me. I was surprised. And proud. I settled into my seat before they could change their minds.

"'Come, sit, *campari.*' Uncle Pete waved the two to the table. He stood half a head taller than any other man in the room. A big, bluff, city boy from Palermo, not far removed from his rural roots, but street smart before he set foot on the steamer. They took places on either side of him. Ciccolini slumped in his chair, hands in his lap, looking beat. In contrast, Greco stared hard at his tenant and one-time pal, hands resting on the table, clasped firmly. Pappa poured wine into tumblers and passed them around. In a gesture of equality that surprised me because I had never seen such subtlety in him, he simultaneously slid one glass to Chico with his left hand and another toward Carlo with his right. The next went to Uncle Pete - then one for himself and a half-glass for me. I had never felt so important.

"'The room filled with cigarette smoke. The burnt tobacco flicked from the ends of their Lucky Strikes piled up in big glass ashtrays and spilled on the oilcloth. Everyone smoked in those days. Even my mother sneaked a butt every once in awhile, when she thought no one was looking. Everyone but Pappa. His lungs already were shot from the stone dust.

"Uncle Pete opened the sit-down after glasses had been drained and refilled – except for mine – and room temperature bumped up four or five degrees. All of us were sweating."

Maxie launched into his rendition of the sit-down, complete with accents, inflections and gesticulations, taking all the roles. He was James Cagney, Robert DeNiro and Al Pacino rolled into one, with a liberal dose of George Carlin and Jerry Seinfeld.

"'So, Greco, you think Ciccolini don't treat you right?' Uncle Pete said.

"'*Padrone.*' Maxie assumed a formal, subservient tone. 'I pay good rent, I keep the place clean, I do good business. My customers they go next door to buy fruit and vegetables from Ciccolini.'

"'And they come from his store to yours. You think Chico can't do with his property what he wants?'

"'Not this way. He gives me one month to get out, find a place…'

"'But your family can stay living upstairs, no?'

"'Where can I go?'

"'Don't whine, friend. It's no help. You have a piece of paper, a contract?'

"'No. We shake hands. That's all. That's enough.'

"'Maybe yes. Maybe no.'" As Maxie mouthed the words he held his palms up in front of him and waved his hands in a gesture of ambivalence, at the same time angling his head from side to side for emphasis.

Maxie as Pete turned his attention to the grocer. "'Frank. You like that better than Francesco, yes? What is your word worth? Do you need a rent paper between *paisani*? You want to bring the law? The Irish cops, the redneck sheriff, the *Alleman* politicians? Are these people your friends? Do they invite you to the courthouse for coffee, for bourbon from the bottle in the drawer? Does your wife go to the mayor's house for tea and cookies with his wife?'"

"'Don Pietro, not yet. Someday, yes. Already they come to buy beans, lettuce, apples, grapes... I give them good quality. Good prices.'" Maxie spoke the greengrocer's words with a faint accent, reflecting his advanced assimilation.

"'The fresh stuff from the market? Prices better than you give to me, to Giuliano? Not the bottom of the basket? A little bit wilted greens, soft tomatoes?'

"'I have to build my reputation. Nobody complains what I give them. I need the butcher shop for wholesale. I can get school business. *Ristoranti*. In this country we live like these people, the good life, not *la miseria*.'

"'How long before you get this new business from your new countrymen? Tomorrow, next week, next year?'

"'Maybe. I don't know. I need the room.'

"'What does it cost you to give your neighbor more time? To let him support his family as you do yours? To let him have a piece of the - whatchamacallem - apple pie?'

"Ciccolini looked at his shoe tops, afraid to make a commitment. Uncle Pete pretended to lose his temper."

"'You! Both of you! I am ashamed you bring this to me. So I tell you what you do. Frank, you give Greco six months to find a new place. You cut the rent five dollars a month. You help him find a store or a good job. Carlo, get off your backside. Help yourself. Help your *paisano* with his new business. You can trust each other more than all these *pezzi novanti*, these big shots, downtown.

"'So, put your arms around each other. Do what I tell you. I'm gonna watch what you do every day. You, boy, Mario, you are my assistant. When I don't go to the store, you go.'"

"Then Pete broke into a rough laugh and dragged the adversaries into a sweaty three-way hug."

Griggsbie interrupted. "So, how did it work out?"

"Not too badly. As it turned out, Greco wasn't all that good a businessman and he ended up going to work for another Sicilian, Ciccolini's competitor in the produce business, who had even better connections and a bigger business."

"And Ciccolini...?"

"Made a fortune in real estate. He had big ideas and a short attention span. Gary Ciccolini, the title lawyer, is his son."

"And Mario Giuliano, boy assistant...?"

"I was fascinated by the way Uncle Pete got them to do what they should have done in the first place. He had an uncanny sense of people, especially our people. He was scary sometimes. He taught me that justice is a communal thing. If you can define the community... More and more difficult every day, isn't it? ...then you can get acceptance of the process and the consequences."

Maxie paused, drifting, and raised his eyes to the framed certificate that said he was licensed to practice law in the Commonwealth of Kentucky. "Where was I?"

Griggsbie, a star reporter because he was an excellent listener and observer, chose not to answer his friend's rhetorical question, to let him flow on.

Maxie picked up the thread. "Anyway, I also learned that justice is administered by an elite, no matter whose system you follow. It's just like history is written by the winners. I became bound and determined to become part of that elite.

"After Carlo and Frank had left and Pappa got a coughing fit and went to bed, Uncle Pete kept me in the kitchen for another hour."

CHAPTER THIRTY

"Pete let the fire go down and the tobacco smoke clear out. He poured me another half glass of wine and told me to sip it slowly, enjoy the taste, feel its warmth. '*Vino*', he said, 'is not to get drunk, but to make a hard life easier.'

"'Those two *paisani*, they are good people trying to change. Ciccolini is smarter. He's changing faster. Greco is a more simple man. He has a good heart but will always follow others. We have a saying in Sicily. 'A man born round does not die square.' Some people think it means you must spend your whole life where you started. It's – what you say – a put down for poor people. Not so. It means a man is who he is. Get to know a man. What he does changes. How he acts changes. Who he is does not change.

"'All of us came here to America for change. Why would we come here if we had it so good in the old country? Life was miserable. Nothing you see here on Jefferson Street is as hard as the best we had in Sicily, your pappa's people in Calabria. To come here is to put on new faces, different clothes. Everybody who got off the boat wanted to buy an American suit with the little money they had. I left the old Pietro in Palermo in a back alley. But I use the same head, the same arm to be the new Pete here in Kentucky. I am who I am but I am also who I have to be.'

"'Remember, Maxie, you have many people inside of you: good, bad, dark, light. You have to live with all of them. You can wash your face but not your soul. What is important is that a man controls all those people. Our way is to keep inside what we do not want others to see. Trust yourself, your family, your people. You never know everything about someone and they should know about you only what you want them to.'

"It was the first time he ever called me Maxie. I was surprised, because he respected my father and always called me Mario in his presence. He knew then what I did not, that I had deeply hurt my father by abandoning his father's name."

"'Tell me, boy, how much do you know about your father?' That question came out of left field, like he was reading my mind.

"'Not much', I said, "He's not a big talker.' We both laughed at that.

"'Let me tell you some things about this round man who is your pappa- *la storia*.'"

Griggsbie squirmed, crossed his legs tightly. Maxie noticed. "You need a bathroom break?"

"No, no. Go on. I'd rather piss my pants than miss this."

Maxie as Pete took up the string. "'Nato Giuliano, the stonemason from Calabria, a place of rocks, goats and poor people. When he was fourteen his family sent him to Naples to cut the stone and send money home. He never saw them again. After Christmas in 1908 the earth opened up and swallowed the whole village. More than a hundred thousand people died from the earthquake in Calabria and Sicily.'

"'He walked all the way home in the bitter cold and nothing was left. No people, no houses, no nothing. The *Carabinieri* sent him away. One soldier poked a bayonet in his ribs. As you say, he got the message.'

"I said to Uncle Pete, 'So, what did he do then?'

"'What do you think he did?' I didn't dare answer. Just asking the question was stupid.

"'Well, boy, he kept his mouth shut and slept in a cave that night with people like him who lost everything they owned and everybody they loved. I can't tell you how he made it back to Naples, but he did. He almost starved to death. He didn't want to do nothing he was so unhappy. His *padrone*, the boss who took him to Naples the first time, found him scrubbing floors and cleaning toilets in a sailor bar on the docks. It was truly *la bella fortuna*. The good luck. The *padrone*, called Gabo, needed stonecutters for Vermont in the United States. Your pappa could not say no.'

"I asked him. 'How did he get to Kentucky?'"

"'Patience, Maxie,'" he said. "'Long journeys take time.'"

"'Sixteen days on the ship to New York he had the seasickness then a train to Barre, Vermont. Two years it took him to pay back the '*mrigan padrone*'. He ate a lotta *pasta fazool* and baloney sandwiches.

"'Nato was a hard worker and he loved the granite stone. So good with the mallet and chisel kept him out of the sheds, where the dust killed men in a few months.'

"I interrupted him. 'Doesn't Pappa have dust in his lungs now? That's why he coughs so much and spits blood.'"

"'Could be worse, son, a lot worse,' Pete said.

"'He minded his business and learned enough English to get along. He told me he never liked Vermont or the Yankee Doodles, what he called them. In the Depression he lost his job and reached out to Gabo who got him work here making buildings. Later he went to work with the Scotsman cutting stone for the cemeteries. There was a few Italians here. He boarded with my mother. That's how he met your mamma, Desideria Vittorino – Daisy. Nice, huh? He needed somebody to cook, clean house, make babies. She needed to be respectable. Nine months later, out pops little Mario. I think you know the rest, eh.'"

Maxie breathed deeply and slumped into the chair. Griggsbie reached over and flicked of the recorder. Both knew the interview had ended.

"So, Griggsbie, that's as much as I can tell you about my father and how I became a lawyer. In one generation I brought the Giulianos from the dust and rocks of a ruined Calabrian village to influence and prosperity…"

…and in doing so, I have no one to pass it on to. The thought was unspoken, but the very thinking of it blunted what he had said aloud. The reality of it made pointless all that had gone before. If famiglia lay at the core of his identity, then he had failed, and in his heart he judged himself a failure.

"One more question. Off the record. Just for me. What happened to Uncle Pete? I haven't heard you talk about him in a long time."

"I'm not sure what to say. With the passing of my father, Uncle Pete and I grew closer for a while. He was always on the move. When not looking for the next deal or keeping a low profile, he would disappear for weeks on end, usually to Las Vegas or New Jersey. He went to Sicily a couple of times. He gave me his contact information, just in case. I never asked in case of what. We agreed that I wouldn't know any more about his business than I had to. So far as I know, Pete has never been arrested or charged. I guarantee you I would find that out."

For the first time Maxie seemed to hold back. His speech lacked the passion with which he had delivered the replay of the sit-down.

"Pete left town not long after my mother died. I heard from him once. A girly postcard from Las Vegas. No return information. A few weeks before he took off he got jammed up when he tried to collect a welched bet from one of our upstanding local constabulary. I took care of the beef but Pete was non grata afterwards. He and I had been drifting apart for a long time before that. Maybe I grew up."

If there were more it went unspoken.

Maxie swiveled his chair towards the door. Griggsbie wanted more. But the visit was over and his bladder could hold out no longer. The story he had come for would await another day, one he was sure would come, but not today.

Griggsbie let himself out. The heavy outer door clicked shut and locked.

CHAPTER THIRTY-ONE

Griggsbie gone, Maxie rearranged stacks of paper and closed a volume of Southeast Reporter Second on a page marked with a yellow Post-it note. The session with his reporter pal had not gone well. He felt vulnerable and, for all his skills, there were some things even the most accomplished actors could not hide. He reached for the universal remote control on the right corner of the desk and aimed it at the 19 inch TV-VCR sitting on a credenza opposite his desk.

He rewound the tape to a familiar mark on the counter and pressed "Play." It was *2001- A Space Odyssey*. The scene is the computer brain control area of the spaceship *Discovery*. Dave, the sole surviving crewman, is pulling memory blocks from the computer Hal's program storage area. Hal has killed all the other crewmembers and tried to take control of the ship from Dave.

As Dave dismantles the computer's brain, Hal continues to speak in a monotonous drone, trying to dissuade him.

Hal cajoles: "My mind is going. There is no question about it. I know I've made some very poor decisions recently, but I can give you my complete assurance that my work will be back to normal."

He pleads: "I'm afraid. I'm afraid, Dave."

His memory almost totally gone, Hal regresses to the time of his earliest programming and recalls a song taught him by his first programmer. He continues talking to Dave, becoming increasingly child-like.

"If you'd like to hear it I can sing it for you... It's called Daisy. 'Daisy, Daisy, give me your answer do. I'm half crazy all for the love of you...'"

Hal's voice goes off-key, slurs and slows, deepening, like a record played at an ever-diminishing speed. Finally, all his memory units pulled and floating in the weightlessness of the brain room, he goes silent. The image on screen is of Dave going to an area designated EMERGENCY POWER AND LIFE SUPPORT. He flips some switches and lights go on.

Maxie hit the "Stop" button, then "Power". The set went dark. A phone rang down the hall, breaking the stillness. Maxie pulled the chain on the antique green-shaded desk lamp. He sat there for a few moments, washed in the fluorescence of the waiting area's ceiling fixtures flowing through his office door, then picked up the handset and punched seven digits into the keypad.

"Hello," a woman's hoarse, boozy voice interrupted the ringing. Maxie's delay in responding drew an irritable "Hello, who is this?"

"Leah, it's Maxie."

Momentary silence, then a terse "Susan's not here."

"I know. She's spending the night in Lexington. I wanted to talk with you. I need to see you."

"See me? What the hell for?" The words were hard-edged and sharp, daggers hurled through the line.

"I want to come over this evening. I need to talk to you." Maxie's voice was firm but gentle, a plea buried in the words, although he pointedly did not ask for permission to visit.

Leah scoffed. "You need? That's new."

Then, in a more amenable tone that betrayed her curiosity, she said, "What do you want to talk about?"

"When I get there. One hour? That's seven-thirty. You still like fried fish and turtle soup? I'll bring supper."

"Okay, big spender. If you want beer, bring your own." She hung up without saying goodbye or letting Maxie reply.

Maxie's mouth twisted in half grimace, half smile. He was uncharacteristically conflicted, unsure of exactly why he made the call and what he would say when he got there. He hummed a familiar tune as he walked to the parking garage.

CHAPTER THIRTY-TWO

Inside the narrow foyer of the Old Highlands Tudor, Maxie held out in his right hand two white paper sacks, a fried fish on rye bread and Styrofoam bowl of steaming turtle soup in each. The gesture signaled an offer of peace. A six-pack of Heineken in bottles hung in his left hand. He had not been in that house in several years, the same number of years since he and Leah Wycov had exchanged anything more than a few strained civilities.

A stern-faced Leah took the sacks and led Maxie to the kitchen. Neither spoke. They were resuming in silence something begun long before and interrupted, incomplete, more bitter than sweet. Maxie had the foreboding sense of entering a hostile courtroom. He noted Leah's trademark needlework, hanging in frames on walls, embroidered on throw pillows and stitched on geometric pieces of fabric displayed on chair backs and tabletops. Leah shaped her world through the messages she sewed on cloth. Set free, those words took on the authority of holy writ.

In the kitchen, Leah placed the food on a counter, her back to her uneasy guest, and took down plates as Maxie set the beer on the table. He hung his rain soaked coat familiarly on a hook inside the back door. There he recognized with a cynical shake of his head Leah's yellowing paean to herself: "*God could not be everywhere and therefore he made mothers,*" gaudy in peacock blue block letters. He recalled he first saw it shortly after the birth of Allan and Leah's second boy and it had since informed all visitors who was in charge.

Maxie returned to stand beside the table and rested both hands on the back of a chair. Leah positioned and repositioned the sandwiches and the soup containers on the countertop and clattered eating utensils in a show of activity. "So, Goy Boy, you need to talk to me?" She spoke matter-of-factly, not turning around, the ethnic barb a remnant of their youth, when she so badly wanted his attention. It was also a reminder of a barrier that stood between them.

If it wounded him, Maxie did not let on. "Yes, I did say that. Maybe I've made a mistake."

He spoke partly from genuine self-doubt and partly with the deliberate intention of testing her receptiveness. The first clue to her mood had come from the needlepoint hanging on the wall beside the refrigerator, impossible not to see from where he stood. The image was of a serpent being ground under a woman's heel. The aphorism, "*A Snake Deserves No Pity,*" was one of many received from the mouth of Leah's Polish Bubbe, her mother's mother, whose dour nature Leah had inherited. He was certain she had mounted it there after his call.

Leah faced him across the room and leaned against the counter. She lit a cigarette and as she exhaled the first drag her words rode on the smoke spilling from her mouth and nostrils.

"The only time we ever seek each other out is when something bad happens. Since I'm just sitting in the same old shit pile, I guess it must be your catastrophe this time. What you got, Maxie, a hangnail?"

Leah's callousness chilled Maxie. He was slow to respond as he processed the likelihood of her having heard something about his health, or that she was just belittling him and his reason for being there. He scraped the chair away from the table and angled his body toward the door. Maybe he should not have come here, not sought something he should have known he might not find.

He resigned himself to finishing what he started, a matter of necessity, of pride. "Something like that. It's a brain tumor, actually. Not malignant. But they can't do anything about it, either. I wanted you to know. There aren't many people I can talk to, who would care."

Leah threw up her hands. She railed at him, her brittle self-control crumbling. "You remember the first time you came to me like this? It was when you found out your precious Uncle Pete was *shtupping* your sainted mother. Your world was shattered. You had to tell me then, too. Why me? Why do you bless me with these revelations? You think I care? I can't do a goddam thing about them and I ran out of sympathy a long time ago. What do you want from me, Maxie? I can't help you! I'm not a doctor. I'm not a priest. I'm not your wife. You feel pain like the rest of us. You just think you're God."

Leah's aim was deadly. Fair or not, she spoke from her heart, in pursuit of setting things right, bordering on vengeance. The line between justice and revenge was a thin one and not at all clear to the target of her vituperation.

She was right. Years ago, Maxie had desperately sought her out, as a friend, as a woman to whom he could vent his outrage and sense of betrayal. He had just won the "Chollie Booz" trial and could not wait to tell Mamma, the one whose approval he most needed and wanted. It was a Wednesday afternoon. His mother's market was locked, so he let himself in by the sidewalk door to the stairs leading to their flat above the store. Good, he would surprise her. He opened the upstairs door, expecting to find his mother in the kitchen. It was empty. Hearing sounds from her room he rushed through the apartment, eager to hear Mamma's praise. Through the partially open door he saw Daisy stretched across the bed on her back, her skirt pulled above her waist, and Pete between her outspread legs pumping furiously and grunting like a rutting boar.

Stunned, Maxie retreated in shock and shame. As he fled, he heard his mother cry out in her passion words that were never to leave him: 'Ah, Pietro, *innamorato*. Harder! Harder!'" It was brutal irony that the person he would next have told of his triumph was his street-wise mentor and buddy, Uncle Pete.

That was what he in his anger and confusion had laid on Leah that night. She lived alone in a small apartment carved from a stately Old Louisville townhouse. She had consoled him to the extent she could. He spent the night on her sofa. He never told anyone else what he had witnessed – nor did he confront the two people once dearest to him, whom he most trusted. He never again looked at them in the same way as before. That he masked his feelings was a tribute to his histrionic talents. He was sure that was not the first time and had probably been going on for years even before his father's passing. His father, the simple stonemason with leather hands and tissue paper lungs.

Young Maxie's illusions of sanctity, of the inviolability of family, had been shattered. He could sweep up the shards and hide them away, so long as he never looked at them again.

Maxie did not defend himself, instead he went for Leah's weakness, in the same way she had just gone after his. "It's Susan, isn't it? You can't forgive her or me because she's working for me. A lot of water has flowed under our bridge, but that's one thing you can't let go of. She's too good for what I do and I'm not good enough for her!"

Leah started forward, her eyes slitted, and opened her mouth to speak.

Maxie cut her off. "You want to throw stones? Here's one for you. She loves what she's doing and she's damn good at it, and we both resent the hell out of your trying to manipulate her. She can speak for herself, but I'm telling you the problem is you, not her or me." Maxie's response was as calm and measured as Leah's last words had been sharp and spontaneous, which served only to stoke her ire. "And one more thing, *Bambina*, we're not sleeping together…never have, never will."

The woman lunged furiously towards him, spouting obscenities. She had strained to bear his assault but broke when he spoke the taunting nickname of her childhood.

Maxie kept his courtroom face, resisting the urge to smile at her loss of control. He knew when he had gained an edge never to spoil it by gloating. He tensed, prepared to circle the table, to keep it between them. But Leah aborted the charge as abruptly as it had begun, gripping the back of the chair opposite where he stood, mirroring him. They stared at one another, game pieces anxiously awaiting the spin of an arrow to signal the next move.

Leah suddenly let go her grip and tapped the back of the chair with her fingertips. "Enough, Maxie. I'm not sure I want you here. You have your reasons. So, why don't we at least try to keep it civil."

They had got in their jabs, each knowing the other's hot button and eager to push it. It had gone on this way for more than fifty years.

Once they had been lovers, briefly, if having spontaneous and need-driven sex could be called love. It was by far their most unsatisfactory relationship, one they would never speak of, not even now. It had happened at the confluence of her greatest vulnerability and his misguided sense of obligation. Allan had died in shame and Maxie intervened with the Bar Association and Allan's clients to settle his affairs quietly, preserving his friend's reputation and saving the family from financial ruin and social disgrace.

Maxie had used up a considerable amount of his store of good will and secretly contributed more than one hundred thousand dollars, while arranging for and guaranteeing loans that Leah had over the years repaid. Leah knew few of the details and would surely have resented the extent to which she might be indebted to him.

His mother's death a few years earlier had left an emptiness in him that he had not been able to fill. He mistook his sympathy and sense of duty towards Leah for something deeper and far less honest. Their enforced closeness led to disastrous intimacy, something he and Leah had long avoided. He couldn't give enough and she couldn't get enough. He held back and she wouldn't stop pulling, until the tension became so great that the attachment forged between them snapped, leaving ugly, almost palpable scars. The result was, predictably, to reinforce her sense of victimhood and isolation, which deepened as she aged.

None of this would he ever disclose to Susan and, so far as he knew, Leah had kept it to herself. No good could ever come to any of them from Susan's knowing.

"Sometimes, Leah, it's just good to clear the air. I know you'll be honest - brutal, but honest. And it really is too late for either of us to apologize for the past. You have your world. I have mine. But I have to say this: Susan is a precious gift, don't spoil it! She's on her own mission, just like you wanted for yourself and have to accept for her. Let go. I'm not fortunate enough to be a parent, but I've helped a lot of young people improve their lives. Maybe it's not having a father's responsibility that lets me succeed. I get to pick and choose my projects. Real mothers and fathers don't."

"That's right, Maxie. She's my daughter, not yours! I'll never accept that what she's doing is good for her. You're as selfish as you accuse me of being. You are winning this battle. I only hope you lose the war. She deserves better. She's too good for the people she's helping. She's too good for you. But the more I say the farther away I drive her. That makes me even more unhappy. I'll die believing she's made bad choices for her life. And I'm not blind about her social life. It breaks my heart she's not married. She doesn't even bring boys around to meet me. She goes out of her way to reject promising candidates. If I still believed in God, I'd pray for her. I'd pray it's not because she's attracted to women. That would kill me. I can't even bring myself to use that word in the same conversation as Susan's name." Leah caught her breath, ending the rant.

"Now, Susan's no longer up for discussion. You needed to tell me you're dying. Like I said, 'Why, me'? You blew me off a long time ago. I appreciated what you did after Allan left things in such a mess, but that's no more than you would do for a lot of people, not just 'Poor Leah!' So, if you're staying, sit!" Leah swept her arms downward in a final commanding gesture.

"I'll make coffee."

Maxie broke a slight grin. He sat and folded his hands on the tabletop.

"You ambushed me with the snake sampler."

"I knew right where it was. I know where they all are. That one I made a long time ago. You know what they say about the shoe fitting…"

Maxie had set himself up for that one. "Where's my favorite? You know, *'Don't be too sweet lest you be eaten up'*. Your mother told me in your Bubbe's version there was a second half to the proverb."

"What do you mean? That's all there is."

"On your embroidery, yes, but you always ignored the rest of the saying: *'Don't be too bitter lest you be spewed out.'* You make a great editor but a lousy reporter."

"That's the way you always see things, Goy Boy. You have to fill in all the blanks, make sure of every detail."

He saw in her eyes that he had gouged too deeply again. Polarity was their common flaw. Each carried a negative charge into the relationship, and, true to the laws of physics, they repeatedly succeeded in repelling one another.

Leah got up from the table to bring coffee, just finished brewing. "Still take yours black?"

Maxie nodded. She poured two large mugs, white ones with Louisville Bar Association logos, handing one to her visitor and taking a sip from hers as she sat back down. More memories.

"That reminds me, what ever happened to that hand towel you put up in Jerry's room when he was about thirteen?" Maxie wasn't sure what about the coffee mugs made him think of this.

"You mean, '*A half-truth is a whole lie*?'" She didn't hesitate an instant. She knew immediately what Maxie meant. "I still have it, folded in a drawer."

For the first time since he had arrived the corners of her mouth curled upwards in the faintest hint of a smile and her eyes brightened. Her words took on a sweeter tone.

"That's the one. Jerry was always trying to get around the rules. Every time you caught him, he would weave an elaborate story that had just enough truth in it to be plausible. He just never could get past your bullshit meter. Like when you found the girlie magazine under his bed and he said it belonged to Herman Gold, who found it on the sidewalk. You found out that he and Herman had bought it together and were sharing it with their buddies. You got tired of fighting him over each episode, so you embroidered that towel and hung it on the wall in his bedroom. He would take it down and you would hang it up again. That must have gone on for a year. He told me all about it. In his version, he wore you down."

"For the record, Jerry finally got the message. I knew what he was doing, he knew I knew and I knew he knew I knew. If he snuck around, I would find out. I'd listen to his cock and bull then wave the towel in his face. His father just sat back and enjoyed the contest. It did no good to ask Allan to talk with Jerry. He just shrugged and said 'Boys will be boys on their way to becoming men.' I'm convinced to this day Allan coached him, as much to get my goat as anything."

Leah could never admit she was not the victim of someone else's manipulation. The curtain she stitched around her made her impervious to that kind of thinking.

Maxie and Leah reconciled without resolution, without forgiveness or any need to forgive. Each had spoken and each had been heard. The reason for his coming disappeared into their shared history. Leah's faith in her righteousness was unshaken. Maxie suffered no regrets.

Uneaten fish and soup cooled on the counter top. The unopened beer bottles sweated a neglected pool of condensate on the table.

The unabating rain pelted Maxie as he dashed to his car at the curb. He did not look back, did not notice the lights at the front of the Tudor house go dark before he started the engine. He pulled slowly away onto a street empty of human activity.

CHAPTER THIRTY-THREE

Susan recorded the message and snapped the mobile phone into its cradle, hoping her friend would get the message in time.

"Andie, I'm a wreck! Meet me at Rowlie's about seven."

She had decided to spend the night in Lexington and start fresh the next morning. Maxie had been at an all day hearing before a Federal judge and she would call him later. Nothing she could tell him would surprise him, anyway, and he was certain to tell her to get a good night's rest and start fresh in the morning. She smiled involuntarily at the humor of her anticipating Maxie's reaction. He was a good teacher. For her part, she was as good a student and earlier that day had applied his lessons of patience, deference and humility.

The hearing before Judge Benny Willards had been brutal. In a display of his rancor and the power of his office, the judge had heard a full docket in the morning and adjourned for lunch, leaving Susan to sweat out a long wait. She could not afford not to be at the courthouse when he returned. Her midday meal was a can of diet soda and a package of cheese crackers from a vending machine. The hearing convened at two thirty, four and a half hours after it was scheduled to begin.

With Thornburg leading the charge, the prosecuting attorneys had all but accused her of engineering her client's escape. The judge heard her out and expressed bitterly his sense of betrayal, coming within a hair's breadth of summarily calling the $2,000,000 bond posted by Jasper Dowd, who mercifully was out of the country. Jock Dowd had stood mute as far from the judge's bench as he could without passing outside the bar. He had no stomach to put his body between Susan and the blistering tirade Bennie Willards would unleash. Both father and son would have agreed, however, that finding Joseph and returning him to custody was a duty and a necessity, and no one doubted the resources law enforcement agencies would commit to the task.

Capping off the hearing, Judge Willards had craned his bony neck across the bench, and, fixing Susan in a hawkish stare, promised to personally see that she never practiced law again and went to jail if it turned up that she indeed had had anything to do with the defendant's elopement.

Susan spent the rest of the afternoon with Jock Dowd and Jeannie Ann and Eddie Khalil trying to figure out how Joseph got away and where he might be, without success.

In an act that could be seen only as deference to Jasper Dowd, the man to whom he was beholden for his judicial sinecure, Circuit Judge Benny Willards had released Joseph on a two million dollar property bond secured by the Dowd properties. The other conditions were an electronic monitor and restriction to the boy's home and his uncle's law office. If his lawyers needed him to prepare a defense, they would have to come to Parkersburg. The prosecutors, most vocally Albert Thornburg, had objected vehemently, arguing perversely the risk of bodily harm to the defendant because of the adverse publicity and alleged high level of emotions against the accused child killer. It was a position comically inconsistent with their aggressive opposition to removal of the case from Wheeler County for those very reasons. For all the good to be said about lawyers' roles in the judicial system, their facility in changing positions to suit the issue, the client, the phase of the moon, exposes their dark side.

Susan and Jeannie Ann had double-teamed the old man, using every personal and professional argument they could contrive, ultimately prevailing only after the daughter broke down in tears, angrily accusing her father of harboring ethnic hatred as her husband had done just days before.

Now it was looking like they had all been complicit in a very bad decision.

The crowd at Rowlie's had thinned by the time Susan arrived. To her relief, her dear friend was sipping a glass of white wine at the bar, chatting up the young male bartender who was making no pretense of his interest in the good looking blonde. The two women embraced warmly and moved to a corner table where Susan ordered a very dry double Stoly Martini up.

"Okay, girl. Do you have to get drunk before you tell me why you're so strung out?" Andie's concern was real. This was not like the Susan she knew so well.

In very few words, punctuated by angry tears and more profanity than she had used in a long time, Susan recounted Joseph's disappearance and her reaming by Judge Benny Willards, aided and abetted by the selfsame Albert Thornburg whose rudeness Andie had experienced a couple of months earlier.

"You know me, I keep it all together, but my whole world seems to be going to hell right now. I thought I had the perfect situation with Maxie and a great opportunity taking on this murder case. Now the case is blowing up in my face because I haven't got a clue what my client is up to. I thought I had earned Joseph's trust and respect, but he hasn't treated me that way. Every time I meet with him he seems more interested in my boobs and my ass than my advice. I even caught him once trying to look up my skirt when he ducked under the conference table to pick up something he dropped – on purpose, I'm sure.

"Even when we get him back and I'm sure we will – law enforcement is all over it – it's going to be that much harder to defend. Jumping a $2,000,000 bail isn't exactly a sign of innocence."

"Take a deep breath, Suze. Another double for my friend and a house Chardonnay for me." Andie reached across the narrow table and took Susan's hands firmly in hers.

An hour later Andie pulled into her parking space at the condo complex, an exhausted and seriously inebriated Susan slumped next to her. They had chanced leaving the lawyer's rental car overnight in the restaurant's parking lot. Inside, Andie hastily brewed a pot of coffee while encouraging Susan to get into the shower.

"I'm OK!" Susan said in repeated denial. Reluctantly, and with her friend's help, she undressed and stumbled into the shower, letting the hot water stream over her, rubbing fragrant body wash into her skin. She wanted to wash away not only the surface grime but also the guilt and sense of failure that seeped from deep inside.

Andie wrapped Susan in a giant terry towel as she stepped unsteadily from the shower, and rubbed her dry while guiding her into the bedroom. They moved awkwardly in tandem, Andie behind, in charge, fending off her friend's insistent protests of self-sufficiency. Given their history, it was a stark reversal of roles.

"It's okay, baby, let me take care of you." Andie said, with overtones as sensual as they were maternal. Susan responded by leaning heavily backward, into a tightening embrace.

"God, Andie, this has been the shittiest day of my life. I don't want to see or talk to anybody for a month!" The words spilled out in a boozy drawl not unlike that of her mother, only softer, less self-pitying.

At the edge of the bed, the covers already drawn, Andie slipped the towel from Susan's shoulders and let her gently down as a mother might lay an infant in the crib. Susan turned away from Andie onto her side, set free from earthly cares. A marble statue could not have lain more still. Her freshly scrubbed skin exhaled the purifying scent of jasmine. Andie tucked the duvet snugly around her vulnerable friend, as if to seal out the demons of the night, while sleep within dispelled the anguish of the day. She bent and touched her lips lightly to Susan's cheek, affirming the covenant of care to which she had committed.

Taking time now for herself, Andie undressed, showered, put on a terry robe, and in the kitchen brewed and poured a mug of chamomile tea. Gathering her legs beneath her on an overstuffed chair, she cradled the mug in both hands, gathering her thoughts, sorting her feelings. Struggling with the adverse effects of a bitterly shattered marriage, she yearned for stability, tranquility – warmth. Over the years Susan had been her dearest friend, a sharer of confidences, a source of strength to shore up her frailty.

For the first time Andie sensed herself the stronger of the two, the one to comfort and heal. But with this feeling came the unsettling desire for physical and emotional intimacy, so long absent in her life. Could she bring herself to make an overture? How would even the subtlest suggestion be received? Was it really a line she could cross? So much was at risk.

Introspection and the soothing infusion brought her to the point of slumber. Warmed to her depths, smiling serenely, Andie uncurled her body from the chair, padded across the kitchen, and carefully placed the empty cup in the dishwasher, her every movement catlike, purposeful.

Andie entered the bedroom in the dark, dropped her robe to the floor, and slipped beneath the sheets beside the sleeping Susan.

CHAPTER THIRTY-FOUR

As the search for him went on, Joseph hid just yards away from where he had been confined, under the literal noses of his family. The Dowd homeplace had been laid out in the late 1700's atop a stone foundation that encased a dirt-floored cellar. Renovations over the years had expanded and fortified the foundation as wings and stories were added. Plumbing, wiring and ductwork had been installed and updated, furnaces and water heaters placed and replaced, many times. Elaborate drainage channels had been dug to relieve the pressure of ground water against the outer walls and to control as much as possible the dampness inside. Sections had been isolated. The old coal bin, added early in the 20th century, had been sealed up for years.

When a small boy, before his parents built the "little house," an adventurous and inquisitive Joseph pried loose a plywood panel patched across a corner of the abandoned chamber. The space had been scrubbed clean and planks were laid across the rough concrete floor. The opening was just large enough for his body to slide through and there he hid when he could. Whether a tribute to his stealth or plain luck, his hideout was never discovered and, as he grew in both size and guile, he improved his lair and enlarged the entryway. He could enter the cellar either from the house or by way of the heavy storm doors hidden by overgrown privet hedges in the side yard. The original chute opening, a heavy cast iron door, had been welded shut and covered with a layer of facing stone to simulate the original foundation.

It had been at least four years, when he was about twelve, since Joseph had been there. Around that same time he began to play "Dungeons and Dragons" with a vengeance - first as a board game, then on a computer. The only person with whom he had shared his secret, his indulgent and secretly conspiratorial maternal grandmother Libby, always "Grandmother," had passed away not long before.

The ankle monitor had been ridiculously easy to disable and remove and the escape from his parents' house simple to stage. In the dark of night he left a messy, visible trail across the broad lawn to the road then made his way up the middle of the blacktop about a mile, turned back on a gravel road, through a dense copse and back along a gully to the storm doors at the back of the main house. It had taken him nearly two hours and his trail would be hard to follow. He accurately forecast that it would appear he had either hailed a ride or had an accomplice waiting to drive him away. Dogs would be confused on the road's surface. The big house was empty. Jasper Dowd was traveling in Europe and would not return for several days. Joseph correctly predicted that the last place law officers would look was right under their noses.

Although forbidden as a condition of his release to access the Internet, Joseph had appropriated the laptop computer he had set up for his mother. It had the software he needed and a dialup modem. The laptop disappeared underground with the boy.

In his grief and out of respect for his late wife, Jasper Dowd had left undisturbed her sitting room and small library off the master bedroom they shared. He took upon himself the weight of guilt for his infidelities, which he had confessed at about the same time she contracted the "wasting away" sickness that led to her death. Miss Libby had had her own telephone service installed, free of the constant traffic that tied up their home line. The line went unnoticed after her passing and had not been disconnected. The household expenses, which Jasper Dowd had never bothered with, were paid by a secretary at the law office, a secretary who, over the years, had ceased asking questions about the amount or purpose of the invoices she handled. All the household phone charges appeared on the same monthly bill and were routinely approved and paid with no more than perfunctory review. It was into this line that Joseph tapped, accessing servers all over the world to route his connections into EEMOO.

The next statement for Miss Libby's phone would be prepared and delivered to the Dowd Law Firm long after the information it contained would be of use to those who searched for the fugitive boy.

CHAPTER THIRTY-FIVE

Within an hour after setting up in his cellar hideout, Joseph emailed Susan a message in plain language. The text shorthand he and his contemporaries used would have been lost on her and Maxie.

"You won't find me. Alfart won't either. You can watch my trial though. Call Vincent. He'll show you how. You're a good lawyer I guess, but I don't need you or your boss. Tell my mom and dad I'm all right and know what I am doing. They won't believe you. They don't have to. There's a lot of things I'm not sure about. Did you know that Saladin's real name was *Yusuf*, Arabic for Joseph? See you in court. :-)."

Vincent Martin fidgeted nervously at the keyboard of his laptop computer, clicking furiously with the index fingers of both hands, perched at the edge of his chair, intent on the text characters filling the screen. His pallid face glowed in the screen's glare, endowing his thin, sharp features with an elfish look. He had arrived in Louisville from Connecticut in late morning of the day Joseph would be convening his virtual trial, bringing with him the computer program that would allow him, Susan and Maxie to access EEMOO.

Vince in many ways played his friend's alter ego. They met at Remson Academy and grew their friendship as cofounders and role players of EEMUD, an Internet community dedicated to fantasy combat on the Holy Land battlefields of the Crusades, the medium and the milieu of Joseph's obsession with his ancestry. When their interests changed from warfare to social fantasy, they became co-gods of the EEMOO, creating spaces where they could be people they wanted to be, act in ways that pleased or suited them, without need to answer to parents, teachers…or anyone else, for that matter. It was a thrill to build their own virtual world, to set the rules, to change the rules, to break them. As time went on, however, they, especially Joseph, endured the pressure and the judgments of other gamers who joined EEMOO seeking the same liberation and immortality that came with the almost infinitely variable identities that could be assumed and discarded at will.

When Joseph was flamed and exiled from the community Vince chose to depart with him, in part voluntarily and in part because of the taint of association. They turned over the domain's files and codes to Melchizedek, the avatar of an eighteen-year old MIT junior named Levi Bar Reilly, who had come across the "Evil Eye" MOO accidentally while researching the mysteries of the Kabbalah. Melchizedek assumed the role of the god or, as he preferred to be called, the high priest. The titles carried no religious significance; they merely signified the status of the one who controlled the domain.

So it was to control the means of his judgment that Joseph Khalil returned to EEMOO, setting and reserving the right to reset the rules to suit his purposes.

```
Wildalin:   Saladin's back
Greenmonk:  Yer ass! :( We flammed him out a year ago
```

Brendolin: Wonder what he wants Weirdooo

Greenmonk: I'll halve him with my broadsword…

Saladin: You bunch of losers… I came back to give u a game to play IRL

Francoise: CREEP

Saladin: Don't scream at me or I won't let you play

ArtooB4: u never followed the rules before y shoud we care?

Saladin: Im building a courtroom. We're having a trial.

Melchizedek (High Priest of the MOO) enters:

    u r not welcome here, Saladin. Leave us be.

Saladin: I'm taking over for two days. U r going to try me for murder.

For several minutes, no activity was recorded on the screen.

Over the next twelve or so hours Joseph constructed a courtroom in the domain. It was, eerily, down to the water stained plaster walls and worn plank floors, a textual replica of the Wheeler County courtroom of Judge Bennie Willards who, in those same hours, seethed at the prospect of not having the double murder trial of Commonwealth vs. Joseph Khalil take place in his physical courtroom. The fifteen foot high ceilings were edged with golden-hued red oak moldings, of a like color and grain as the wainscoting that rose three feet up the walls, circling the room. The judge's bench, flanked on the jury side by the witness box, rose above all other features, stained dark, almost black with age. Below and in front were the tables behind which sat the parties and their lawyers – at their back the railing that separated them from the public. The public seating area, as the jury box, however, contained no chairs and, in a way possible in a virtual world, could accommodate an indefinite number of persons. Jurors and spectators would be any players in the EEMOO who chose to participate.

Those wishing to pass on Joseph's guilt or innocence needed only to log on. Each player could engage in multiple roles, as a prosecutor enabled to ask questions, a juror empowered to hear the evidence and render a verdict or a spectator. Joseph would play judge, defendant, defense attorney and answer all questions in the personae of witnesses. The fictional witnesses would be two teen-age boys who would say they saw Saladin at the murder scene but did not see the two little boys, the Deputy Sheriff who found the bodies, and the medical examiner who performed the autopsies on the bodies. Joseph's answers as a witness would be the truth as the prosecutors knew it, as the official record showed it . Appropriating the protection of the U.S. Constitution, he invoked his right as the defendant not to testify.

Otherwise, Joseph typed in his own rules of procedure:

"Every member of the domain, including newbies who join the trial before it ends, is eligible to play. Do not presume innocence or guilt. Each player can ask any question of a witness and any answer is admissible. Each player is equal to every other player with one vote for guilt or acquittal. The judge can make any ruling he wants to at any time. You can vote at any time in the next 48 hours unless the judge ends the trial sooner. At the end of the trial, the judge will consider all the votes and decide what will happen to the defendant Saladin. The judge is not required to announce his decision."

A legend, a parody of the *Magna Carta*, was posted above the huge wooden doors through which everyone except the judge entered the virtual courtroom.

"No gamer shall be condemned except by the judgment of his peers, or by the rules of the game."

The rules were, of course, Joseph's rules, and Joseph's peers were the role-play gamers who chose to participate. As master of the game he occupied the position of first among peers.

210

Beyond these bare requisites, there were no rules, no other protections, no instructions. If not a totally new, then certainly a different jurisprudence would prevail.

More than most, in a community where nonconformity is the norm, he became the evil "other". It may have been his refusal to follow the rules of gods and wizards as well as the corollary tendency to make up or change rules on the fly, as they suited him. In this he was consistent and predictable; his direction and motivation, however, were not. Only he had a vision of the order to come from the chaos he generated. And that vision was subject to change at any point along the way.

When he had finished building and furnishing the virtual courtroom, Joseph set in motion the trial proper.

The boy had retained the files and codes that enabled him to take charge of the domain, despite his relative youth, twelve when the EEMUD came into being and fifteen during the transition to the more social EEMOO. Joseph had been a founding wizard and writer of the EEMOO programs. Against the protests of Melchizedek, the god he displaced, and others whom he had offended in past fantasy lives, he shot a figurative bird, [;,!,,], a symbolic "screw you". The possibility of emoticons extended far beyond the simple "smiley face :-)" that started it all.

It was the promise of a new adventure, however, that got the gamers' attention. It would be, he promised, a two-day adventure after which control of the hijacked domain would revert to Melchizedek. MUDDERS were, if nothing else, suckers for novelty and new challenges.

Maxie and Susan – who was suffering the consequences of too many vodka martinis the night before – squeezed beside Vince, looking on in fascination. "What the hell is he doing?" Maxie said. "All I see is a bunch of words."

"Right, Mr. Giuliano, the software turns those words into objects and actions. The courtroom has real dimensions and the players come and go like it was a real place. Each time you see a name that means someone is saying or doing something.

"Like, there. 'SophieT asks a question: Wat u c Saladin do on the bank?'

Witness Teenage Boy answers: Stand on bank looking at me. Then he turn around and walk away.'"

After a few minutes of this it became obvious to Maxie and Susan that Joseph was just parroting what the prosecutors had disclosed to them. "So, Vincent, do you think Joseph will answer any questions about whether he killed those kids?"

"Dunno. He says he won't testify as the defendant. But he can change the rules whenever he wants."

"We're in for a long night, aren't we? From the look of things, this will be pretty boring."

"Not so, Susan, look there." Vincent pointed. Text was flashing furiously across the screen. Multiple players were typing – saying – derogatory things about Saladin in abusive language – bad grammar and spelling aside. "Those are the geeks that flamed him off. They hate his guts."

Suddenly, the laptop's screen went blank.

"What happened? Can you get it back?"

Vincent typed a long sequence of characters but nothing happened. He rebooted the computer and repeated the keystrokes.

"He locked us out. I don't know what's going on in his head."

"Can he do that?"

"Oh yeah. He's not a wizard for nothing. That program is sweet. He wrote most of the code. I helped him but…well, I'm not him."

Susan turned to Maxie, openly disappointed. "Should we pack it in? I'm not keen to camp out in front of a blank screen. You were right yesterday. We're totally out of it. We can only hope somebody finds him soon."

"Vincent," Maxie said, "do you know where he is? If you do, or if you can locate him, we need for you to do it now. No games. This is very serious. You could be guilty of a crime yourself."

"I would if I could, but I already tried. It'd take more than this wimpy box…" He pointed to his laptop computer.

The question would persist whether Joseph's creation was a life-like game or an extension of real life. It depended on who was supplying the answer and from what perspective. Like life itself the line between fantasy and reality blurred. It was beyond the experience or the competence of his pursuers even to know what he was doing, let alone to interpret it. His skills permitted him to use "gophers," Internet applications that could bring text to a computer from servers anywhere in the world, to log on from locations that were untraceable. Yet he wanted Susan and Maxie to know what he was doing and, yes, "that retard Thornburg, who thought he was so freaking clever." They probably felt cheated not playing their roles as the defense attorney and the prosecutor. Saladin was in charge!

CHAPTER THIRTY-SIX

Trying to understand what his absconded client was about, Maxie called in Ellwood Pomffrett, Ph.D., a University of Louisville professor of sociology, expert in the developing customs and "common law" of the Internet. He sat in one of two well-used leather chairs facing the lawyer's desk. Susan occupied the other.

Maxie quickly got the meeting under way. "Thank you for coming Dr. Pomffrett. I won't keep you very long but we have a situation that requires your expertise. I want to know what the hell is going on with my client that he jumped a two million dollar bail and is setting up his own trial on a computer. It makes no damn sense to me what he intends to accomplish and he is royally screwed. Not to mention that he has made me and Susan look like fools or worse. You know he let us watch his show for a few minutes, then shut us out. So we have nothing for you to see. Susan, you gave him the information he needs?"

His associate pointed to a folder the consultant had taken from his briefcase and set on the desk in front of him.

"I'll try, but truth be known I've never heard of anything like this happening and it absolutely fascinates me. It will make a great case study. I assume from what I've been told that you have no experience with Internet communities and role-play games? Is that so?"

Maxie looked over at Susan, Mac PowerBook at the ready in her lap. "She's is pretty savvy, but I can't even use a computer. I have always prided myself at being up on what's going on in the world, but this is so far out I couldn't see it with a crystal ball."

"Some of this you may already know but I'll begin with the basics. Interrupt me anytime.

"Your client has chosen to try himself in a virtual community where a body of common law is just establishing itself and will be only as effective as its members are willing to accept it and conform. Its legitimacy arises from the consent of the community, and doesn't need to make sense to you or me or depend upon our approval. By rejecting a jury trial under the laws of Kentucky, Joseph Khalil is attacking the judicial system. He's saying 'I can get justice or fairness only within a community of which I acknowledge myself a part and whose rules I have a hand in shaping.' And those rules are situational, fluid, still being written.

"Actually, he is playing in both systems. He will expose himself in the virtual world where you have no influence while hiding in the real world. He believes he can decide his own guilt or innocence and mete out punishment in his fictitious courtroom. In the state's criminal justice system, he can play games with the process, mess over his own lawyers, the judge and the prosecutors, but ultimately cannot determine the outcome.

"He has set himself up in something called a multiple user domain, or MUD, which is a computer program that permits people to interact with one another over the Internet from just about anywhere in the world. At this point we aren't able to access the site, but I have enough experience to explain what is probably happening and how it came about. Their communication is entirely text based. There are no pictures. Everything is typed from a keyboard. A computer program displays the characters on the players' screens and allows them to interact. A master – sometimes called Wizard or God - controls the domain, setting, enforcing, interpreting and, as needed, amending the rules.

"These domains are inhabited mostly by males in their teens and twenties, who have expectations, not always reasonable, not always agreeable to others. They assume fictitious identities, play roles, hence the label for what they do: "RPG", role-play games. And within their defined limits they want to exercise the full powers of the creatures they choose to be. Remember, this is a fantasy world, limited only by imagination, and that covers an immense range of possibilities. To paraphrase, the character you see is not what you are getting. It is merely a representation, what we call an avatar.

"If players become dissatisfied with their avatars they can change identities and return in another form, or freely leave. If others become dissatisfied, the offender can be 'flamed', in other words ostracized, forced to leave. An expelled player, whatever his previous status, could be restored to the community, but this rarely happens. The independence and anonymity inherent in the system allow, perhaps encourage, these people to be unforgiving. This is what happened to your client. His peers judged that he had transgressed beyond tolerable limits and threw him out.

"This is the part that troubles me most. I'm a sociologist, not a psychologist, so I see things in a communal rather than an individual context. This young man appears to be seeking redemption from the very people who have rejected him. And he has retained the objectionable persona of Saladin."

Susan interrupted. "I want to hear more about the technology. How are we able to see this happening? And what's going on that we can't see?"

216

Pomffrett obliged and shifted his emphasis. "MUDs started out as platforms – computer programs – for adventure RPGs. The prototype is Dungeons & Dragons, a medieval themed adventure game involving player characters and magic that migrated from board to computer play. Actually, in one version the "D" in MUD stands for Dungeon. This particular MUD is called a MOO…

"…It's okay to laugh, Mr. Giuliano – sometimes I have a hard time keeping a straight face when I teach a class or give a talk on this.

"The original MUDs involved conflict and were played out mainly on battlefields and as castle sieges. The MOOs – so called 'Object Oriented MUDS' are programs where the players engage in more conventional social interactions in 'rooms' or spaces they construct with words. 'Object oriented' means typed characters are translated into people, places or things, including emotions, which are capable of acting or being acted upon. Each player takes a name, describes himself, and acts in certain ways. For example, 'John is a six foot four, blond, blue-eyed body builder. John enters the recreation room and says hello to Jane. John looks sad. Jane smiles and hugs John.'

"The real John may be a fourteen year old pimple-faced bookworm enjoying a virtual life he couldn't have in the real world – 'IRL' in their language. Jane could be a twenty year old male college student having a good time putting people on to see how far they will go trying to impress 'her'."

"Back up, Doc. You're confusing me on this identity thing."

"Mr. Giuliano, let's take what you must already know about fictitious identities, way beyond aliases, when people can't see or hear each other. Like the child porn cases. For all I know you've defended some of these guys. The pervert and the cop trying to catch him both play roles. Each one disguises himself as someone else, an assumed gender, age, occupation. They're role playing, but with real world intentions."

217

Maxie snorted. He had had enough talk. "MUDs, MOOs, shmoos, cops, perps, pervs, wizards, lizards, avatars, schmavatars, whatever! With all due respect, Doc, this sounds like so much mumbo jumbo. Hell, I got the mustard, now you get to the meat. I need to know two things. What does this tell me about my client's state of mind and what is he really risking? Which gets me to a third question. How can we find him and get him back into the real world, where Judge Bennie Willards and I live?"

"I can tell you I don't know what he'll do next. Neither does he, in a way. Kids like Joseph Khalil believe they are in control, but lack an inner compass, a sense of conscience. His senses of responsibility, of accountability – even to himself – are unformed. He may let this so-called jury of his peers render a verdict and then determine what should happen next. As much as this fascinates me, it terrifies me. He's playing with his real life. It's a virtual trial seeking a virtual verdict that could have real world consequences. Other than that, his mental state is outside my field."

Maxie interrupted. "So, tell me how to find him and I'll go get him and see that he doesn't hurt himself."

"I'm afraid I can't help you there, either. I can address only what I have studied and observed, and help put it all into context for you. I'm sure law enforcement agencies are working on that. In all candor, however, these young men are way ahead of even the FBI in both technology and know how, so you'll probably have to wait until the boy decides to come in."

Maxie held up a well-manicured hand in a gesture of surrender. He wanted to hear no more. "I apologize if I appear rude," he said, standing up and walking around the desk. "I'll tell you, nothing makes much sense to me anymore. I've got this 16 year-old kid that's making my life miserable. I'm good. I'm the best. I've worked every angle the system will allow. I know what to say, how to say it, when to say it. I can pick a jury as well as anyone. But for one of the very few times in my life I don't know what to do next. If this is a case of first impression for you, consider how it's affecting me. I've handled capital cases all over the country, for all kinds of criminal defendants, in the weirdest circumstances you can imagine. This one is so far outside the box…" Without completing the sentence, he handed Dr. Pomffrett a check for the agreed consulting fee and saw him to the door.

Pomffrett had confirmed and expanded on what Vince Martin had told them. What Maxie had heard he could understand intellectually, but could not accept at its most fundamental level. Maybe mortality was catching up with him in more ways than one. He had not yet told anyone except Leah about the tumor, about his death sentence. Now he was presented with fantasies of alternative lives, of death and resurrection at the will of the creature. Of gods and wizards. He found himself wishing he could lose himself in that world, where he could slough off one life and choose another. But what other life could he live? For a brief, frightening, moment he actually welcomed the tumor that would release him.

A fascinated and increasingly anxious Susan had absorbed all of this with untypical restraint. She had no difficulty comprehending Pomffrettt's explanation of what was happening, and more than ever felt the urgency of finding Joseph before it was too late. Her problem was that she wasn't sure when too late would be or what it would mean. And, contrary to the expert opinion just received, she was not ready to concede that Joseph Khalil lacked a sense of direction, even though he might lack conscience.

Susan felt compelled to put a cap on the day. "Mr. G, this is a lot more complicated than Joseph just wanting a fair trial on the murder charges. He's got a ton of other factors weighing in. I mean, I think he's rebelling against a lot more than just the legal system."

Maxie cut her short. "Look, all the bullshit aside, we have to get him back. This little game of his will not resolve his guilt or innocence, and that's all I care about. But what do I know? I lost control of this case a long time ago."

CHAPTER THIRTY-SEVEN

They gathered to meet Joseph at The Point, where his message to Susan had said he would be, on the shore near the undergrowth where the mutilated bodies of Billy Ray Patton and Junie Millington had been found.

The river flowed steadily by, its waters fed by early autumn rains. The shallows had deepened, no longer still. Debris along its banks had washed away or submerged in the current. The floodplain was going dormant. Duller hues of the lower spectrum – fading crimsons and dusty ochers, muting to umber – were displacing the vibrant greens and radiant blooms of summer. Shed leaves blew and huddled together in moldering piles. Here and there crops of detritus poked through the receding ground cover and thinning brush. Hints of must and decay floated on the misty air. Wisps of cloud unfurled like lengths of tinted gauze overhead.

Old Judge, hoary in the rays of the rising sun, presided sphinxlike from the opposite shore.

Susan Wycov, Eddie and Jeannie Ann Khalil, Dale Carnahan and Vince Martin made their way from the road through the culvert onto the salient, past naked brambles that snagged their sleeves and nicked their flesh. They called out Joseph's name in a cheery chorus as they hurried on. The boy had specified who should come, down to Carnahan, the only adversary whom he respected, admonishing Susan to not disclose his return to Thornburg or Judge Bennie Willards. As master of the game, he continued to set the scene and dictate the rules.

They spotted him, sitting upright, legs stretched toward the water, his back to them leaned against a willow tree whose wispy branches fanned the air around him. The rays of the morning sun split past the willow's trunk, hiding Joseph in shadow. His left arm rested atop a black laptop computer, his loyal companion of the past few days, the cover closed, lying beside him on the sodden ground. He did not respond to their calls.

Joy turned to dread and their voices rang more shrill.

Vince and Susan raced ahead, sounding "Joseph! Joseph!" struggling to keep their footing on the scraggy plain. They reached the tree and froze in horror at the sight of Joseph, his head enshrouded in a plastic bag taped snugly under the chin. The lifeless mask, eyes bulging, lips spread in a triumphant smirk, glowed a ghostly green in the flickering reflection off the river's surface. The silver and turquoise amulet, given by his Palestinian grandmother to ward off the evil eye, hung impotently at the end of a gold chain around his neck. Whatever its powers, it had failed to protect him from his inner visions.

Vince gaped in stunned disbelief, giving way to Susan, who pushed past him toward Joseph's body. As the young lawyer, tears streaming from her eyes, reached to yank away the bag, the commanding voice of Stubby Carnahan pulled her up short.

"Stop! Don't touch anything!"

The deputy forced himself in front of the others to feel for a pulse. Turning to look directly at Eddie and Jeanie Ann, he gave a shake of his head and reached for the radiotelephone at his waist.

A keening wail exploded from the mother's mouth, "No! No! No! He's not dead! Let me hold him! He's not dead!"

The physician held his struggling wife tightly, preventing her touching the cold flesh. His own grief he let out in soothing whispers of comfort and a sibilant prayer in his native Arabic, invoking the name of God, *Bismallah*, and beseeching Mercy, *Rahmah*, for his departed child and himself. Fallen away from his faith, he prayed the embedded fragments of childhood without ritual. In anguish he turned his eyes to the clay from which his son's soul had departed and fixed his gaze upon the oval blue-green stone, another artifact of his youth. Breaking the palliative cadence of prayer he angrily cursed the superstition and sorcery embodied in the charm and the fantasies and false illusions they spawned.

At Carnahan's insistence Vince and Susan moved several feet away down the riverbank. The boy fidgeted and glanced nervously about at everything but his dead friend. Susan by contrast stood as if rooted in the plain, clasping her face in her hands, and could not take her eyes off Joseph's death mask.

Vince broke the agonizing silence. "Susan, does this mean Joseph killed those two little boys?"

It was a question that swirled in the mind of each witness to the horrifying scene. Eddie and Jeannie Ann Khalil held firm to the belief their son was incapable of such a crime. Carnahan, ever the law officer, saw it as an admission of guilt. Vince, the fellow gamer, thought it his friend's final role-play. A bewildered Susan blamed herself for her client's death and could not answer the question.

CHAPTER THIRTY-EIGHT

The EMT tried to quiet the man as he prepared a syringe of morphine to ease his pain.

"Lord, I got to tell somebody. I got to say my piece. I know I'm a-dying."

"Later, buddy, we'll get you fixed up first."

Matthew Patton threw up an arm, warding him off.

"No, you got to listen to me! I was out back and Billy Joe come runnin' up to me scared lookin' and hollerin' 'Somethin' happened to Junie! He's bad hurt, Daddy! Hurry!'"

The EMT gave in to the futility of calming the raving man and let him rattle on.

"I went fast as I could behind the boy down the river. I seen that little baby lying there not movin' and the blood comin' out of his head and that rock layin' there beside him and I knowed what happened and I grabbed my boy up and started shakin' him. All the time he's hollerin' 'Daddy, he messed his pants! Don't, Daddy, please! I didn't mean to hurt him just throwed a rock at him when he run off!'"

A wrenching sob interrupted the torrent of anguish pouring from the man's mouth.

"The more he hollered the harder I shook him 'cause he's screamin' and cryin' like he don't know what to do and I'm yellin' at him to shut up and then I let go and Billy Joe falls down and he stops hollerin' and I tell him to stand up for his whippin' and he don't move and I reach over and he's like a rag doll and ain't breathin'!"

Patton's voice hoarsened as he gasped for breath.

"I killed my boy, my Billie Joe! Lord, I'm so sorry."

As Patton struggled to continue the tech pressed the needle into his arm.

"You know what I mean. Lookin' up at me like...and me thinkin' that's my sister's boy dead there and that's my boy and I don't know what to do, so I picks them up and hides them in the scrub by the water so nobody'll find 'em and I can get me away from there and oh, Lord, I'm so sorry! I'm so sorry! Sweet Jesus, I'm so sorry!"

Patton faded into incoherence as the narcotic stilled his brain.

"Didn't mean to...you know what I...wouldn't mind me. Killed poor Junie...shittin' his pants, somethin' bad...his daddy...nobody to blame."

Patton went slack, like a tire going flat.

He whispered weakly, "Gimme a smoke."

Whether Matthew Patton thought he was dying or not, his life was not in imminent danger from his injuries. The techs called ahead. He would be treated then taken into custody. At some future time he would be charged with the death of his son and his wanton tossing of Junie's still live body into the underbrush where feral dogs would devour him.

It was there all along, the truth, the answer hidden just below the surface. The prosecutors had fixated on Joseph very early on. He was the easy target, tainted as much by his own erratic behavior as by the circumstantial evidence building against him. Thornburg crafted, then peddled, the story that was easiest to sell, that a fearful public was most likely to believe. And to his enduring shame he succeeded, although not in any way he intended.

Susan and Maxie were still dealing with Joseph Khalil's suicide earlier that same day when Susan received the news. Perhaps this knowledge might have made a difference. Perhaps not. It was something that could never be known.

Patton had disappeared soon after his son and his nephew were buried. His absence was commonly attributed to the devastating effects of the deaths on a personality already shown to be unstable and unreliable. Without him, however, the last person known for certain to have seen the children alive besides the suspected killer, a crucial part of the case was missing. A part now known that changed everything – a part that Joseph Khalil could not have factored into his self-ordained trial and self-execution. But all now knew what Joseph had known all along – that he had not killed the two little boys.

Maxie and Susan had intended to offer up Matthew as having opportunity and means even though the available evidence pointed strongly to Joseph. Motive was going to be problematic. What he might have done to his own son, always a possibility, didn't mesh with the death of Junie Millington. It would have been a tough sell to a Wheeler County jury. However, they needed only to raise reasonable doubt in the jurors' minds. Too late for all of them, it became clear that Matthew Patton would have cracked when questioned.

The reactions at the Commonwealth's Attorney's offices in Louisville and Parkersburg were mixed. The local team expressed dismay and relief, though without the feelings of loss and remorse afflicting Susan Wycov and Maxie Giuliano.

So certain had the prosecutors been of their primary suspect's guilt, validated by his flight, they had ruled out others early on. The Khalil boy had opportunity, means and didn't need a motive stronger than a perverse and demonstrable desire to take life for the pleasure it would bring him. In their scheme of things, Patton was on the victim side of the ledger. His concurrent statement to Sheriff Tellis had been believable, although clouded by shock. He had said he last saw the boys when they took off just after supper and hadn't seen anything to arouse his concern for their safety.

Stubby Carnahan had reached Thornburg just before six in the evening with the news of the accident and the confession, relayed to him by a State trooper buddy familiar with the case. Thornburg received the news as a disaster and refused to take calls from anyone, including Parker and Simmons, or to talk to the news media.

Thornburg had not told his colleagues Patton had called two days before, to say he was coming in. The man's speech was slurred, often incoherent. At times he screamed about justice being done and the killer getting what he was due, then he would sob, muttering regrets and begging forgiveness for what he had done. By the end of the conversation, Thornburg wasn't sure whether he had heard a father's plea for vengeance or a confession to something more than just being irresponsible. The prosecutor quickly came down on the side of his own rectitude. There was, after all, Patton's history of instability and fecklessness. He said he was calling from a bar and had clearly been drinking heavily.

Thornburg's certainty was abetted by his desire to best Maxie and Susan by convicting their client. On the one hand, he had welcomed a face to face with Patton before going to trial in the hope that his case would be strengthened. On the other, he had no desire to discover the father's complicity or at the very least hand the defense an alternative theory from which to argue reasonable doubt.

Joseph's actions absolved everyone – the investigators, the prosecutors, the judge, and the defense attorneys – from responsibility for the outcome. They had been drawn into the game the boy constructed and played, the rules he set, the judgment he rendered.

What had begun in broiling August with the deaths of two mothers' sons had concluded in the damp chill of October with the death of a third. Tragedy bred travesty as the pursuit of justice went astray. And travesty in its turn brought forth more tragedy.

CHAPTER THIRTY-NINE

Rebecca Millington received the news of Joseph Khalil's suicide with cries of vindication - that justice had been done and vengeance delivered against the evil imp of Satan. Such closure as that may have brought was hollow and short-lived. Stubby Carnahan arrived unannounced at the Millington bungalow in early evening of the same day to break to Rebecca the news of her brother's confession. Sheriff Paul Tellis was a hundred or so feet away at the rundown trailer, telling Corly Patton how her son had died.

Rebecca did not want to accept that the deaths of the two little boys could have happened that way. A demonic act of double murder would justify her suffering. Instead, it was the Patton curse of ill temper and worse judgment, the black cloud that hung over their family.

"Do you want me to take you to the hospital to see Matthew?" Carnahan made the offer out of concern and compassion. He was unprepared for the vehemence his good intentions incited. Rebecca's wrath exploded in his face.

"I hope he dies, the miserable little bastard, and burns in hell! Those little boys will be looking down on him from heaven and they will have to forgive him 'cause I surely never will."

Then, just slightly more in control but with unabated fury, she said, "No, I want him to live a hundred years and remember what he's done every day of his worthless life!"

EPILOGUE

The adolescent voice broke the grim silence.

"You know, I went to that place before, when I was nine or ten. I remembered the gully that leads down from the road, with the briars on one side and the outcrop on the other. It's where runoff drains from the road. I notice those kinds of things. A man that worked for Grandfather took me there fishing once. I never knew exactly what he did; it seemed like he just hung around the stables and sometimes hauled stuff in this old blue pickup truck. They called him Dander. I remember whenever somebody would say something that bothered him he'd get this funny look on his face and say 'Don't get old Dander up.'

"I pestered him for a ride in that truck and he finally said okay, that he was going fishing over at The Point, on the river near where he lived, and he'd take me if I didn't tell anybody. Like, he was skipping work and I wasn't supposed to leave the farm. He had some poles in the truck bed buried under a bunch of dirty canvas.

"He was kind of a rough guy, you know. Like, he cussed a lot. And soon as we pulled onto the road, he got a bottle of whiskey from under the seat and started drinking. I don't remember being scared because I thought nobody who worked for my grandfather would ever harm me. Anyway, he took me out on this part of the riverbank that stuck out in the water. What I remember best is that I didn't like fishing, mostly because it meant getting dirty, and how peaceful it was there. It was kind of grown wild, but the water was still and the palisades just kind of looked down on us from across the river.

"I wandered up the bank while the old man fished. I sat down under this big old willow tree and imagined creatures in the clouds and faces in the bluffs. I don't think he caught anything and by the time we left to go back to the farm he was pretty sloshed. The ride back was scary. Like, he drove really fast and couldn't stay inside the lines and he kept babbling about going to be living like a lord.

"You know, I never saw him again. Once I heard one of the grooms saying it was 'too bad about old Dander, but he probably got what he deserved'. Whatever that was. Like, I couldn't care less."

Maxie and Susan had stopped by the office upon their return from Parkersburg and Joseph Khalil's funeral, to conclude a post mortem begun on the drive back in a flurry of what-ifs. Hindsight was not in this case illuminating. Susan played for her boss a recording of the boy's casual and unguarded narration of his first visit to The Point, taped in one of their earliest interviews. She had not known what to make of it then, and even now struggled with its full import.

Vince and Susan had recovered from Joseph's computer the record of the virtual trial. The hodgepodge of votes, cast by his jury of role-playing gamers, ranged from vitriolic condemnation to compassionate acquittal, with no clear majority. In the end it was not they who decided his fate.

Vince showed her a separate file in EEMOO where Joseph had created a fictitious room in addition to the courtroom that precisely described his coal bin hideout, labeled "My Dungeon."

Maxie comforted his young associate, offered her the wisdom of his years, allowing that the outcome was unpredictable. Despite Dr. Pomffrett's warnings, Susan and he were not to blame. They had fulfilled their duties to the legal system they were sworn to uphold, and to their client, who had chosen his own path to justice.

"I'm taking off now, Mr. G," Susan said, barely smiling, indifferent to his assurances. She stood, smoothed with steady hands the skirt of the funereal gray suit, lifted the black leather trench coat from the arm of her chair, and backed toward the door.

"A lot has happened to me in the past few days and I need to sort it out. Nothing needs doing that can't wait or someone else can't handle, so you won't be seeing me around here for a couple of weeks. I can't say for sure. And no phone calls. I'm going *incognito*." She was not asking permission. Maxie acknowledged her departure with a simple nod of acceptance as she turned and was gone. Alongside the firmness of intention, he had heard in her voice a fatigue and futility he had known many times and now felt again. Perhaps it signaled laying to rest more than just the mortal remains of Joseph Khalil.

Maxie sat quietly, contemplative, muggy palms pressed against his temples to contain the graveling that pounded with each beat of his pulse. *Time to pop more pills!* His detachment from Joseph's case in its last days did little to ease his feelings of bewilderment. This was not supposed to happen to him, to so badly misjudge a client and his case. Did it lie too far outside his nearly forty years of experience? Was it because of the tumor shutting down his brain? Like a judge ruling against each motion, each objection, the throbbing admonished him, portending the final verdict.

Was he so impaired that he had he taken his eyes off the ball? The eyes that were beginning to twitch and blur with a will of their own? He could no longer indulge in the fantasy of denial.

Maybe the time has come to take that trip to Italy.

Maxie had never left loose ends and would leave none now. He picked up the phone and punched in a well-used number. Several rings later a recorded message intercepted the call. After the prompt, he spoke in the clear, confident tones of his vaunted jury summations: "Griggsbie, I'm ready for you to finish writing the story." He replaced the handset in its cradle as precisely as he might reshelve a case reporter numbered on its spine.

Had he a mirror, the stonecutter's son might have seen chiseled in the flesh of his face the *corpus juris* of the life he had chosen. An encyclopedia of mirth and pain, of success and failure, of all the roles he had played – as surely the image of devotion to his calling as were the gnarled fingers carved on Fortunato Giuliano's headstone.

At peace, the legendary barrister rose to go, as he had on so many occasions retired from a courtroom, having given his best, leaving others to deliberate the verdict. He paused at the lobby door and looked back down the fluorescent-lit hallway at the trappings of the world he had built. With a trembling hand he flipped the switch and exited in the dark.

www.ingramcontent.com/pod-product-compliance
Lightning Source LLC
Chambersburg PA
CBHW061136170626
46809CB00003B/882